# EACH
# DAY
# A SMALL
# VICTORY

# EACH DAY A SMALL VICTORY

# Chips Hardy

Illustrated by
**Oscar Grillo**

Published by
**Can of Worms Press**
London

**Each Day a Small Victory**
First Edition

**Published by Can of Worms Press 2007**

Can of Worms Enterprises Ltd
8 Peacock Yard, Iliffe Street
London SE17 3LH, UK

Tel: +44 (0)207 708 2942
Email: info@canofwormspress.co.uk
Website: www.canofwormspress.co.uk

ISBN 10: 1-904104-03-7 (HB)
ISBN 13: 978-1-904104-03-2 (HB)
Copyright © Chips Hardy 2007
Illustrations Copyright © Oscar Grillo 2007

British Library Cataloguing in Publication Data
A catalogue record for this book is available from the British Library.

Edited by Isabelle Hierholtz
Typeset in Adobe Caslon by David Whelan
Cover design by Oscar Grillo on behalf of Can of Worms Design Group

Printed and bound in the United Kingdom

*for*

Mum and Dad.

# Author's Note

I'd like to thank Stewart Wilson for the wildlife calendar he put together so adroitly all those years ago. Mandy Fletcher and Malcolm Gaskin for checking I hadn't wandered too far off the track in search of a joke. Sir Roy Strong for his generosity of spirit. Pete Townsend, Peter Whelan, Robert Lindsay and Sally Emerson for reading and rereading. Isabelle Hierholtz for all her painstaking help with the text. Helena at the Open Book, Richmond for her enduring encouragement. Piers Russell-Cobb for finding Tobias Steed at Can of Worms and both of them for making this happen.

Then of course there's the beloved Oscar, who came from another continent and very probably another planet to share the trenches with me over the years and see this safely home.

Finally, thanks to my wife, Ann, and son, Tom, whose support sustained me through even the most dismal and rainy of days.


*C.H. London. May 2007.*

# Each Day A Small Victory

# January

## Happy New Year

The Roaring Road came from where the sun rose. It cut down through the Oak Wood. Then it cut a straight line through the heart of the wheat and the hay fields and ran right on through to the low horizon where the sun set.

It brought humans in their coughing boxes and it took them away.

Every day coughing boxes streaked down the hill through the Oak Wood, rounded a tight right hand bend and then flung themselves past Max's burdock patch beside a rotting food box the humans had left in a small lay-by. Or else they streaked headlong back the other way, fields on either side, back up into the Oak Wood and out of Max's country.

Usually the humans ignored the lay-by, the rotting food box and Max's burdock patch. Usually they ignored the wheatfield behind the lay-by and the lane just beyond it that led up to the duckpond and the human's green patch. Even though some humans had their burrows up there and there was even a tall, pointed burrow beside a field of tall stones.

Usually the humans ignored the lane just across the Roaring Road, a short run before the lay-by. That lane led up to the Pig Killers, their burrows and their pig fields. (Although, sometimes when it was dark, big coughing boxes that smelt of death would go up this lane empty and come back down filled with pigs squealing in panic on the night air.)

Sometimes, though, a coughing box would pull off into a burrow way much further down the Roaring Road towards where the sun set. This burrow, directly beside the road, smelled of oily and had lights on all through the night. Coughing boxes would cluster there like ants on a run, before charging onto the Roaring Road again and taking off to the low horizon. It was a burrow to avoid. But it, too, was out of Max's country.

And sometimes a coughing box would manage to slow its careening path down the hill and round the bend and bring itself to a juddering halt in the lay-by itself. And humans would get out. And interfere.

And the last thing Max needed right now, in the ravening chill of mid-winter, was a little human interference.

Max was a young adult stoat and the rotting food box in the lay-by was at the hub of his territory, his country. There was no question of that. He'd made sure that the nearest male stoat, Big Dave, an undoubtedly major local figure, was a good hike and a fight away.

If Big Dave did move through his country, Max let him go. For now. But Big Dave generally had other business to occupy him. In different directions luckily.

There were female stoats around of course. Some of them had young, of which none were his so far. But he never really met up with any of them. They might pass each other across a windswept field but, short of a brisk scent for other males, there was no real contact. The time wasn't right for that. Yet.

Max had more important things on his mind.

He was watching Stan the sparrow, his wife Jean and her brother Morris pick moodily at some crumply lying at the foot of the rotting food box. They'd been picking it over for some time now, and still hadn't managed to dislodge a crumb of anything worth swallowing.

But times were hard. And cold. Which was why Max was calculating the distance between Morris and himself, factoring in surprise, the lethargy of frozen sinews and the inevitable loss of concentration that came from long-term hunger. If Max got his take-off right, Morris wouldn't know what hit him.

Stan and his family were a cheerful almost chirpy lot normally. But the mid winter hunger had ground them down, and they had sunk in on themselves like morose little feather bundles. Their minds were on food. Their minds should have been on other feeders.

The birds were having a tough time of it all round. Redwings and fieldfares were lying dead in the fields. Max had found a couple but the crows had got there first and, after that, there was hardly a mouthful of gristle and feather to be bitten out of the hardpacked, icy ground.

He'd even found a mallard long frozen beneath the ice in the duckpond but he couldn't get through to it, and a human's dog from a nearby flower field had come far too close for him to keep trying.

Still the wood pigeons were out setting up their territorial boundaries, cooing out exclusive domains to starve in. And, from time to time, Max caught the sound of Frank the blackbird taking on a thrush under the hedge behind the lay-by over the elusive promise of some ancient wormcast.

It was too cold for even the worms to show. Food was scarce for everybody. Even the owls were hunting during daylight hours and Max checked above him just in case. He didn't want a Tawny homing in on Morris just as he got into the killing stride. But the slate grey skies were empty for the time being.

"Nothin' 'ere at all," Jean puffed out her chest feathers as she complained. "Never should've left the Pig Killers."

"We didn't leave," snapped Stan, trying to ease out a phantom dropping and then realising he hadn't eaten enough in the day to produce one. "That flappin' cat chased us off out of it."

"Flappin' cat wants its flappin' throat bitten out." Morris found that a likely looking crumb of wheaty was in fact a flint sharp sliver of gravel. "Nothin' ere either."

"Keep lookin'." Stan stretched his neck to loosen the ice from his ligaments. "Unless you fancy sortin' that cat out yourself."

"Ha flappin' ha," Morris muttered, but he went back to the gravel.

Max slipped out of his burdock patch, belly flat to the earth. He kept his weight on his back legs, concentrating on keeping some purchase on the icy grass as he eased his way over towards Morris at the base of the rotting food box. He'd need to be able to spring beyond him once the sparrow realised the attack was coming. He'd have to pluck Morris out of the air, before he managed to scrabble into full flight. Or he'd have to go hungry.

He was at the critical point, between the target's awareness and his own muscle release, when a coughing box screamed into the lay-by and skidded to a halt. Gravel and sparrows flew up in all directions.

Max was already back in his burdock patch by the time the door opened and a human female clambered out. She hovered between shutting the door and moving into the shelter of the big hawthorn bush at the far end of the lay-by. The shelter of the hawthorn bush won.

A male human stayed inside the coughing box but he called out through the open door. "I just can't believe you're doing this."

"Don't be so po-faced," the female called as she rushed behind the hawthorn and squatted down in the pale green leaves of cuckoo pint. "Shouldn't have bought me that beer then, should you?"

"Might've closed the door," complained the male. "Freezing in here."

"You're cold!" the female laughed at this, as steam rose up around her.

"There's a petrol station in a mile or so. See it from here."

"Too late now."

Max sniffed the air. He picked up the unmistakable sweet, sour smell. The human female was marking her territory.

This one's spoor was new to him. Indeed the last humans to spray here were a large group of males who had arrived in the dark some nights ago in a big coughing box which smelled of burning leaves and mulched barley. Max had watched as they stood in a line and marked from the hawthorn bush up to the rotting food box. They'd chanted and laughed and burned more leaves and then got back into the big coughing box and moved off into the night.

Perhaps this female had scented those males from her coughing box, and was leaving her signal for them. I move through here. I am in season. Fight for me and I will mate.

"You're steaming like a horse."

"Gentleman wouldn't be looking."

All this was bad news. It meant the males would be back, trying to scent for her. It meant his lay-by would become a mating run. Why didn't she just mate with the male in the coughing box?

The female emerged from behind the hawthorn bush, ran back to the coughing box and clambered in.

"Checked your knickers? Never know what might have leapt in here with you."

"Just shut up and put your foot down. Mum'll kill me if we're late for lunch."

She slammed the door. The coughing box roared and shot out of the lay-by and Stan the sparrow called down to Max from his perch on the rim of the rotting food box.

"Least she's getting lunch."

Max looked back up. Stan knew he'd been after Morris but he wasn't going to say. He wouldn't want to trigger bad feeling. Although nobody had time for bad feelings in these cold, hungry days. Bad feelings burned up too much energy.

Unless you were a crow, of course. Bad feelings were second nature to crows. They thrived on them. Survived on them.

Max watched the crows land with careless ease, as if nobody else was there, certainly no danger. They sauntered along the hard shoulder leading into the lay-by, looking around them with amused unconcern, as if they were waiting for some small joke to present itself.

The crows were brothers, Brian and Ray. And wherever they went they brought menace and the prospect of sudden, vindictive aggression.

Brian, slightly larger than Ray, picked up Max in his chilling gaze almost immediately. He strutted slowly over, resettled an errant feather threatening the perfect line of his immaculate plumage and stared for a disconcerting moment or two into the middle distance directly above Max's head.

Max kept his eye on Brian's murderous beak. He'd seen it break a cat's skull open in one blood-spattering arc. Then Ray had darted in to widen the fissure before the groggy animal had slumped fully to the ground. These brothers were the instinctive masters of violence. They were gifted at it.

Brian cleared his throat. "Hello Max. Lovely day for it, eh?"

"Lovely," answered Ray, who believed a question asked outside the family was a waste of time.

"Get a sniff of anything so far?" Brian was chillingly polite.

They were ravenous. They wouldn't be hustling him for leads if they weren't. Their pride wouldn't allow it.

"Very slow," Max kept the tone light and easy but he

checked his escape route to the battered hedge bordering the wheatfield behind him. Nothing and nobody in the way there.

"Woodpigeons are all over the green patch by the duckpond," Brian observed. "No end of noise."

"No eggs though," Ray sounded aggrieved. The pigeons had let him down. "No young, neither."

"What about you, Stan?" This was the first indication that Brian had noticed the sparrow grasping the rim of the rotting food box. But of course the crow brothers missed nothing.

"I could do a sparrow," Ray conceded. "Need two or three, mind."

"Busy morning?" Brian's voice was a lethal whisper.

"Nothin' about." Fear gripped Stan. He could hardly get the words out. "I'd tell you, Brian. You know that. If there was."

"Who's your Missus with? Under the hawthorn?" Brian could spot a meal through branches, leaves, grass and even mud probably.

"Morris. 'Er brother."

"Oi!" Ray shouted at the hawthorn. "Come on out! Your husband's got company."

Jean and Morris stayed in the depths of the bush. Too scared to call back. Morris managed a less than phantom dropping.

"No way to behave." Ray felt slights keenly. He turned to Max. "That anyway to behave, Max? When your husband's got company?"

"No way to behave," agreed his brother sharply. "No way to behave at all."

Here it comes, thought Max. He'd watched the crows at work before. Always the sounds of outrage and wounded feelings followed hard by the ferocious assault. He steadied himself, to be ready for the atrocity when it erupted. But Stan caught them all off balance.

"Something going on up the Pig Killers though," he blurted.

"Why aren't you there, then?" Brian was icily suspicious.

"Cat ran us off," Stan explained earnestly. "Wouldn't bother you though, would he?"

"I've taken cats." Ray picked at a claw with his beak, then fixed Stan with a manic glint in his eye. "Taken big cats in my time."

"Course you have." Stan nodded his head frantically. "Bigger'n the Pig Killers' cat an' all, eh?"

"So what's going on up there, Stan?" Brian sounded as if his patience was being sorely tried.

"They got the turnips out. Big heaps." Stan was so eager to explain he almost fell off his perch. "For the pigs. All sorts up there now."

"Rats?" snarled Ray.

"Loads. And mice."

"Mice!" sneered Ray. He was too hungry to bother with the smaller rodents.

"Everything you like," Stan cheeped desperately.

"But no sparrows," observed Brian cruelly.

"No. Well. Not as such." Stan sunk down onto the rim. It looked like he'd failed.

Ray stood stock still, a puzzled look clouding his black eyes. "Brian. Do we like turnips?"

Brian turned to his brother. He spoke softly. "Rats, Ray. We like rats. Remember?"

"Rats!" shouted Ray and he gave his wings a sharp flap. "We like rats!"

Ray took fast little steps here and there, thinking about them. And when Brian flexed his wings and took off, his brother was only seconds behind him. They flew in a lazy half circle and then headed across the Roaring Road and off towards the Pig Killers' burrow and the pig fields behind it.

Max watched them go. "There'd better be something up there for them, Stan."

"I know." Stan closed his eyes and gave a fatalistic shrug. "I know."

ℬ

The Duchess lay on one mighty flank; her haughty spirit once a byword in accepted social circles was now all but extinguished with ennui. Her favourite niece, Angela, stood a few feet away at the door of the arc and looked out on the trotting way beyond the front fence.

"Phillipa's down to the turnips again."

"Never one to show any restraint," breathed the Duchess, and she rubbed a great cheek against the strewn straw in sad confirmation.

"Persistent though," opined the Duchess's younger sister, Miranda, who was settled with slightly less abandon in the opposite corner. "Never let intelligent enquiry get the better of her, that one."

"She's turning quite a size, Mum." Angela looked on enviously.

"Bulk isn't everything, dear," replied her mother soothingly.

"Turnips," the Duchess sighed, "and one tries so hard to maintain a vestige of dignity."

"You've worked selflessly, my angel."

"One holds society together by the merest thread." The Duchess breathed out fiercely through her nose, ruffling the last of the potato peelings scattered around her monumental face. "One transcends the ice in the irrigation, the queue jumping at the scratching post."

Angela looked back at her mother and they both cast their eyes quietly to heaven. This was to be one of the Duchess's melancholy days.

"One expects of course to be responded to in like manner. Well, one lives in hope." The Duchess's moist eye caught Miranda's, who instantly put on her dutiful face and nodded sympathetically. "And then they dump vast mounds of turnips in the main trotting way."

The Duchess did not sound surprised. The world was as

dross after all.

"That is an unusually large amount of turnips, Auntie." Angela was forced to agree; although she had sidled down to root through a few earlier in the day, while the Duchess was staring at the wall.

"No order, no courtesy, no consultation, no serving arrangements," continued the Duchess, her great dugs swelling and plunging as her agitation increased.

"And no priority," Miranda voiced the Duchess's main preoccupation for her, like any first rate amanuensis.

"Turnips for all and sundry." The Duchess managed to sound both perplexed and aghast. "All and sundry."

"Especially Phillipa," said Angela spitefully. "If she doesn't stop to breathe every once in a while she's going to asphyxiate herself with them."

Her mother stared pointedly at her. In circumstances like this, it devolved to the Duchess's favourite niece to rescue her mood. Angela took a deep breath and sang out brightly.

"Rowena says the boys have got potatoes."

Her mother turned her face to the wall in despair as the Duchess exploded in spluttering fury.

"Well really! Has that trollop been over by their fence again? Flashing her dugs, straightening her tail! She's in for a surprise, I can tell you."

The Duchess made several heated efforts to roll to her feet while Miranda glared at her daughter with a baleful "Look what you've done, now." scowl. Angela tried to fit herself into a small corner of the little yard outside the arc as her massive Auntie trotted towards her, her dander well and truly up.

The young pig kept her snout to the icy mud as her Auntie snorted into her ear. "You just don't know anything, do you? You and your silly little cousin. You think it's all boys and grunting and having fun in the breeding holes."

Angela lifted her frightened eyes up to the angry sow. "I'm sorry, Auntie."

"It's not like you think, you know. It's twisted round and

round on itself." There was a desperate sadness in the old sow's eyes that her anger could never disguise. "And it hurts. It hurts like anything."

The Duchess stopped suddenly and looked around her, as if she couldn't remember what had brought her tearing into her favourite niece on a chill January day, in front of polite society. She stared questioningly at Angela, and then turned and walked forlornly back into the arc.

"It hurts like anything," she repeated. Only this time it was just for herself.

Angela seized the opportunity offered by the vast behind disappearing into the arc. She darted out into the trotting way and made her way over to the offending turnips and some badly needed social interaction.

It just wasn't fair. Every time she mentioned Rowena, the Duchess went into outraged hysterics. It wasn't her fault that the Duchess couldn't stand her own daughter. And she was going to tell Phillipa all about it.

Phillipa was steadily loading turnips when Angela shuffled up beside her. They flapped ears to ensure Society had registered the meeting was a formal one and then Angela began pushing a turnip round with her snout. She wasn't really there to eat; she was there to exchange views.

"That your Auntie getting the vapours?" Phillipa didn't look up from the task; she had bulk to build.

"Unnerves me when she does that," Angela admitted. "Did you get it over here?"

"Must've heard it in the boys' field," snuffled Phillipa. "And have you seen what it's done to the Pinkie-poos?"

The Pinkie-poos, four new girls from Phillipa's Mum's latest litter, were just out of weaning. This was an early social outing for them and it had ended in disaster. The Duchess's ferocious trumpeting had unsettled them badly. They hid at the back end of the turnip mound, squeaking in fear and standing on each other's feet.

Angela snorted scornfully at them, "Oh get a grip, girls. You'll never bulk up like that."

Phillipa looked up as she crunched through a

particularly resistant tuber. Her eyes slowly focussed on something beyond Angela's shoulder. "Mother's dugs!" she swore indistinctly. "Who on earth let these in?"

The crows had made an entrance. And, as far as Angela could remember, there wasn't a social protocol for dealing with uninvited crows. Society simply wasn't equipped. So she maintained a polite silence and a frosty glare.

Ray missed this completely as he strode sturdily along the turnip line, his beak thrust about him in furious questioning arcs. He paused for a moment to cock his head on one side, and then strode on with renewed and surly disapproval.

"Pigs," he concluded. "It's all pigs."

Brian landed deftly beside him and shook his head before drawing himself up to his full condescending height. "It's a pig field, Ray. You got to expect pigs."

"Rats. You said. Rats." Ray was deeply wounded at this brotherly betrayal. He'd come for rats. All he saw was pigs.

Brian inspected the long mound of turnips. Then suddenly he ran up to the top and stopped. "They'll be under here somewhere, Ray. Just a matter of waiting."

"Very idea!" huffed Phillipa. "He's walking on our lunch."

"Sooner or later one of the Fatties will stand on one. And we're in."

"Fatties." Angela was appalled. "They're bringing Fatties with them. Whatever they are. More mouths to feed I suppose."

"Nerve of some." Pricilla rooted angrily amongst the turnips causing Brian to dodge quickly back along the top of the turnip mound. He soon recovered his poise though and yawned loudly at the sky.

Ray skipped lightly towards the foot of the mound and flicked at something with his beak. "Potato skin. Old bit of potato skin," he called up to his brother. "But no rat."

Miranda appeared at the door of the Duchess's arc and called over, "Angela. Angela!"

Ray looked over sharply at Miranda. Was this the Fatty

who was going to stand on a rat for him? "Don't hang about, girl," he rasped. "There's rats need standing on."

"Angela!" Miranda ignored him and kept calling out to her daughter. "Angela!"

Eventually Angela turned round, rather embarrassed at being shouted to in this fashion. In front of Phillipa and the crows and the Pinkie-poos. Well, everybody really. Mother was impossible sometimes.

"What is it?" she tried to sound as independent as she could.

"Don't encourage them."

"Mummy!" The injustice of it all.

"You're not encouraging them are you? They might go away."

Back in the arc, the Duchess shifted one vast haunch disconsolately, her great head laid flat amongst the packed straw. She sighed deeply before making her world-weary pronouncement. "They've come for the rats."

Her sister turned back to her from the doorway. "Are you quite sure, dear? I didn't think we'd been brought any rats."

⁊ə

Max watched Stan, Jean and Morris back picking though the crumply at the base of the rotting food box. His moment had gone. The crows had made the sparrows far too nervous for a sneak attack over open ground to have any chance of success.

He went through the options again. Another trek round the fields, hoping some vole had warmed up enough to make a foraging expedition amongst the white patches of cow parsley. A probing run under the hedge, in case a younger blackbird was over-occupied with a worm or an older one was trying to breathe its last frozen moments in some privacy.

Experience told him he wouldn't get that lucky. It also told him he had to eat before dark. He needed energy to hunt, and he had to keep hunting to stand any real chance of making it though the night. It was a simple matter of fuel.

So he thought about the pig fields. And the turnips. Somebody leaving food unattended like that would draw in all kinds of unwelcome attention. Worms, the hardier insects, birds of course, and eventually, rats and mice.

Word would have to get round to draw everyone in, but it had been started now with Stan's plea-bargaining with the crow brothers. And allowing for a few more chance discoveries by other foragers up there and the odd, inquisitive rat bringing all his friends back to the feast, the turnips certainly looked a prospect.

He worked over the threats. No problem with the pigs. They'd be too busy feeding and too slow to run any real interference. They just bulked and bulked until the big coughing boxes came in the night and surprised them.

There was just the one working dog, he reminded himself. And another old one that spent every day in a lingering death on some woolly outside the Pig Killers' burrow. One tomcat, vicious but lazy, who'd most probably walk the other way. And the Pig Killers of course. You could never be sure of them, coming out of nowhere.

Wherever you found a human, death could arrive from almost any direction. The only thing you could be certain of was that you'd never know where or how that danger would fall on you.

At that moment Morris coughed and spluttered out a small shred of crumply that he was trying to convince himself was a crumb of wheaty stuff. And Max made his decision.

He stood up on his back legs, and checked around him. Nothing that remotely resembled a meal and nothing that immediately resembled violent death. He was going into the pig fields, Pig Killers or no Pig Killers. He was hungry. That's all that counted. The Pig Killers would have to live with that.

When a stoat gets hungry, it gets nasty. There was nothing he could do about it.

Max sprinted across the Roaring Road.

ৎ৯

Rowena trotted jauntily back towards the turnip mounds with the air of a job well done. She'd cut an attractive figure, pink and plump, in front of the boys in the adjoining field. She'd got them salivating through the fence and shoulder barging each other surreptitiously in futile attempts to look cool and unaffected. She had kindled desire.

And that called for a celebratory turnip or two along with a little worldly preening in front of Angela (such a frumpish little sow) and Phillipa who was positively backward when it came to the opposite sex. Rowena tossed her head back as she trotted and prepared to make a suitably theatrical entrance in the trotting lane.

But as she approached the females' arcs she discovered the limelight had been snatched from her. There was a commotion at the far end of the new turnip mound. Phillipa and Angela and Angela's mother Miranda were all gathered round the Pinkie-poos and staring fixedly into the midst of the turnips. A sleek crow stood on the top of the mound as though directing operations, whilst another dodged this way and that around the unheeding pigs.

As she was not to be the immediate centre of attention, Rowena stood still and watched, waiting to see how to make the greatest social capital from engaging with the situation.

Only, just then her mother made a stately exit from the principal arc and caught sight of her daughter offering her better profile at the start of the trotting lane.

"Don't just stand there like a wart on a frog, Rowena!" she ordered peremptorily. "Something's happening in the social arena and we need to be represented. Even if it's only by a useless lump like you."

Phillipa and Angela were looking over at her with mock-sympathetic smiles and all the Pinkie-poos still had their eyes shut tight in fear. So it was Miranda who gave a short scrabble in the turnips with her fore trotters and a shout of recognition.

"There it is! I saw it. There!"

Rowena walked over sulkily. Being the daughter of the Number One Sow, she managed to cover her embarrassment at her mother's treatment with aristocratic disdain. She stared at the Pinkie-poos who were positively vibrating with terror. "What on earth's got into them?"

"Something's in there eating our turnips." Phillipa's voice was flinty with anger.

"We think it's a rat," explained Angela. "None of us have seen it, though."

Brian poked his beak down where Miranda had trampled, and then called over to Ray. "Can't make it out. You better get in there."

"I'm on it." Ray danced in between Angela and Miranda, checked into the turnips and backed out again. "Nuffink. This old porker's too slow to save her life."

Miranda turned on him angrily, but he ducked back a safe distance and cocked his head to look at her out of one quizzical eye.

Rowena gave the turnips her moody look, "How do you know it's a rat?" Then she looked at Brian with heavy emphasis.

"We didn't invite rats either, did we?"

"Well, it bit a Pinkie-poo," Phillipa added. "So it's probably rabid."

The Pinkie-poos squealed and backed into each other at

the idea and the one who thought she'd been bitten evacuated suddenly, causing a further flurry of anxiety. Miranda quieted them with a snort.

"Stop exciting them, Phillipa. They're daft enough as it is."

"It's rabid now," Angela whispered to Phillipa. "Even if it wasn't when it started."

"We should all stop and listen," ordered Rowena. Social engineering was in her blood after all. "Then we'll fix its position."

Ray walked closer to the Pinkie-poos. They were bigger than rats, granted, but they were in more plentiful supply. But he suddenly found himself face to face with Miranda and he didn't much like the size differential. Or the look in Miranda's eye.

"You're not invited. And you're not wanted. So why on earth are you still here?" Miranda piled on the condescension but Ray had already flapped himself up alongside his brother on top of the turnip mound.

"We'll stick to the rat, Ray." Brian tried to calm the situation. "Now we've started."

And so they all kept silent, even the quivering Pinkie-poos. Angela, Phillipa and Rowena held their snouts inches above the mound surface. Miranda stood looking off to the edge of the field but listening intently. The Duchess sank down in the doorway to the arc and flapped an ear in benediction.

And soon they heard the scuffling from deep inside the mound. Brian adjusted his balance, ready to plunge his razor beak into whatever furry life was scurrying below.

"That's a rat alright." Brian, the expert, nodded at the sounds.

Angela gave a swift rake in the turnips with her right fore trotter and sniffed deeply at the gash. The scuffling continued. The rat, if rat it was, was making its way back up the mound towards the entrance to the trotting way and away from all the prying eyes.

"Rat alright," echoed Ray as he tracked along the top of

the mound, staring down for his dinner, poised ready to throw himself at it. "C'mon out you little flapper."

Phillipa bounced her way through Rowena and Angela and hurried along the side of the turnip mound herself. "That's our rat!" she yelled to the crows. "In our turnips."

"Yes! Go find your own," Angela shouted, and Brian took off to fly down to the far end of the turnip mound. Ray was still sidestepping along.

"Found it?" Brian snapped. They'd have to move fast to take this rat off the fatties on their own ground.

But Ray heard nothing. He was focussed on the kill.

Phillipa overtook him down the mound and waded purposefully into the turnips. If anyone was getting to the rat she was. "Get your own rat, beaky!" she yelled.

Ray scampered back at this invasion and looked askance at his brother. "What she on about?"

Phillipa stood knee deep in the turnips searching around with her snout. Angela and Rowena waded in from either side.

"Are you sure you're happy standing on other pigs' dinners?" The Duchess felt obliged to comment on this breach of protocol.

"Needs must, Mummy," Rowena called over her shoulder.

"Can't let a crow steal our rat after all," said Angela.

"Do be careful, dear." Miranda had rediscovered her maternal feelings in the midst of all the adrenal competition.

Angela looked scornfully back at her mother. "It's only a rat, mother."

At that, the turnips in front of her erupted as a shrieking and thrashing ball of brown fur tried desperately to seek the safety of the skies before being dragged back out of sight. Gouts of blood spurted across the surface of the mound and into Angela's eyes.

Angela squealed and blindly backed away out from the danger. In her panic, she trod heavily on Rowena's foot and the pain drove her friend to thrash her head round and bite angrily into the unfortunate Phillipa's ear. Phillipa screamed and bit back at her, raking at her flanks with her teeth. Ray and Brian were airborne in a heartbeat, staring down at the ensuing mayhem.

Squealing and slashing, the younger pigs scuttled back out of the mound and away down the trotting way, scattering the Pinkie-poos. Phillipa nipped at Angela's leg as she overtook her in headlong flight only to be barged to the ground by a furious Miranda. "How dare you bite my Angela?"

"She started it," wailed Phillipa.

"I didn't," protested Angela. "Something else did. In the turnips."

"There's blood on there."

They all turned to look. But it was quiet there now. The turnips were silent and motionless again.

Brian and Ray landed on the mound beside the bloodstained site of the eruption. They looked long and hard at the drops of blood on the turnips. "Never seen a rat behave like that before," said Brian.

"Not a rat?" Ray was unsettled. They'd all told him it was a rat. Now they were confusing him. A lethal move on their part.

Brian lowered his head and poked at the bloodstained turnip with his beak. "Don't think it can have been. Not with all the wet work."

Max's blood-drenched face appeared momentarily between the flecked turnips only inches in front of Brian's beak. "It was a rat, Brian," he said pleasantly, "but it's not around any more."

And then he disappeared from view.

Ray was incensed. "You ate our rat! I'll beak your eyes out."

Rowena turned to Angela, aghast, "That was a stoat. In the turnips."

But there was no further sign of Max and the crow brothers grew more and more uncomfortable as they stood silently on the top of the turnip mound. Until Brian flapped his wings once in icy fury. "The rest'll have smelt the kill by now," he spat. "Won't be a rat this side of the Oak Wood."

"He ate our rat." Ray was still stunned at the effrontery.

"We'll try the duckpond. Maybe a woodpigeon's frozen up there. Cooed himself to death." And with a bad tempered cough, Brian took off and flew back towards the Roaring Road. And Ray, as ever, was a heartbeat behind him.

And with their exit, the drama seemed to leave the pig field. Miranda ushered the Pinkie-poos into their arc. Phillipa walked peevishly off to hers for a lie down, leaving Rowena and Angela staring at the mound.

"A stoat. In our turnips." Angela shivered at the thought.

"It'll be long gone by now." Rowena saw the question in her friend's eyes. "Well you never see them about do you? Stoats are always somewhere else."

They walked up towards the Duchess who was trying to roll herself onto her feet. "Mummy," Rowena called over, "we think it was a stoat."

The Duchess gained her feet and turned magisterially back into her arc. "Rats. Stoats," she pronounced gloomily. "That's exactly what you get for leaving turnips all over the place."

They watched her bed down heavily in mute contemplation of a world going to the stoats. Then they wandered off up the trotting lane, so Rowena could tell Angela what she'd been up to by the boy's field.

❧

Deep in the heart of the turnip mound, Max curled up by the remaining shreds of the rat and decided to sleep till

nightfall before risking the track back to the lay-by. A rat like this would keep him well fuelled for the cold night's hunting ahead.

On balance it had been an easy kill and so it was now one he could forget. Nothing to learn from it. No new threats to watch out for.

It was important to learn. As the seasons changed and the days lengthened, there would always be different threats and different opportunities to be snatched alongside them. He knew his country well. He studied it constantly but he'd never fully know the dangers it harboured. And he'd never foresee the one that would kill him.

Anyway, his next kill was always the matter at hand – surviving to make it, living through it and using it to move on to the one after that. It meant moving fast and thinking faster still, and then resting up in safety to make sure you were still quick enough to prevail the next time.

And kill led to kill led to kill, which in turn enabled him to rest, to walk his country, to breathe in its smells, to feel the heat and the rain on his back, to scrabble out of the ice or stretch out in the sun. Life could be good between kills, provided you kept one eye out for whoever you were going to pull down next and the other out for anyone having the same thoughts about you.

It was always this way. He was a stoat, one of the Blood and Guts Crew. His life was a precarious series of calculated risks, taken under too much pressure and with too little room for manoeuvre, but exploited with a full armoury of teeth, claws, explosive muscle power and the capacity for instinctive, unbridled savagery.

It would be a long year. If he made it. But that was what he was built for. And he wasn't going anywhere else. Not willingly anyway.

As he dozed off, he wondered whether Brian and Ray had caught up with Stan in some vengeful, vindictive fury.

He hoped not. Stan would come in handy on some other hungry afternoon.

# February

## The Night of the Living Dead

Max loped along under the hedgerow beside the lane that ran from the duckpond and the humans' green patch right down to the Roaring Road. The afternoon sun was pale, the day chill and the light meagre. The hedge itself looked battered and worn down by a relentless succession of wintry days. With a cold night to come Max had a long way to go before he could sleep with any sense of security.

He'd just spent an unrewarding hour in the dwindling daylight foraging through the hazel coppice between the green patch and the flower-fields the humans had made by their burrows. All he'd found there were yellow catkins and some magpies chattering round the bleak remainders of last year's nests.

He'd heard some greenfinches wheezing away in the tree-tops and a human's dog frenzied barking as it picked up the rank scent of a male fox on a mating run. A scent

Max had picked up a long time before, on his way in over the meadow. Foxes were pungent at the best of times but now they were out on the job their reek made your eyes water.

But he'd laid eyes and claws on nothing he could eat.

Running easily, he scanned the hedgerow for sound or smell of mouse or vole but the cool earth just fed back his own light footfalls. Until he heard the dispute up ahead.

"Beak off, you mottled scum-warbler!" Someone up ahead was very angry.

"Scum-warbler? I'll give you scum-warbler!" came the equally outraged reply. "You yellow-faced egg-crusher."

"My hedge! My worm!" returned the first. "Now beak off! While you've still got both eyes!"

There was a scuffling and a drumming of feet. And then a short flapping of angry feathers. Birds, smiled Max. Birds too busy fighting to notice the muted arrival of their last moments on this chilly earth.

He stayed low and inched forward until he came to the next rootclump. Then, keeping his head at ground level, he looked carefully round to see an adult male songthrush with one claw stamped over half an earthworm. He was pugnaciously facing off a male blackbird. The other half of the earthworm protruded from a pecked out hole between the blackbird's feet.

The blackbird had its back to Max, its tail up and its yellow beak flung out at the songthrush in terrible anger. "Fancy your chances, do you? You sing-along tit-sized bug-guzzler!"

The thrush drew itself up in full fury at this affront to his creative capabilities and was about to hurl down some dreadful rejoinder when he focused for a second behind the blackbird's shoulder and saw Max edging gently forward on the hardpacked earth.

"No!" he shrieked, before terror rooted him to the spot.

The moment the blackbird registered the thrush's fear-stricken expression, he knew this change of posture had nothing to do with him. Trying to keep the adrenaline pumping, he swung round to meet the new threat, splaying his feet for a better fighting stance.

As soon as he saw Max, he froze but the bravado of his turn seemed to release the thrush who crashed headlong through the twig curtain and took off. Only when he found himself safely away did he scream out his warning calls.

"Thrush in danger! Danger! Danger! Thrush in danger!" His voice faded away, leaving Max and the male blackbird looking at each other.

Max appraised the distance he needed to cover to make the kill. The blackbird surveyed him out of the corner of one dark eye, his wings outstretched, poised to fly through wood and earth if necessary.

"Sorry, Frank," said Max softly. "Seem to have interrupted your party."

"Full of themselves, thrushes," Frank was quietly scathing, "All song and no egg maker." He stretched sadly then, "You hungry, Max?"

"Pretty hungry, Frank," Max acknowledged regretfully. Regretfully because the blackbird always had a quiet smile for him. And a little comment. A small joke at the great pains of life as it is lived. If you pressed Max he'd tell you he had nothing against Frank. He might even have said he liked Frank. Well, he liked Frank when he wasn't this hungry.

"Not easy these days, is it? Every bounding, crawling, flapping and slithering thing is on the worms now. Same every time it gets short." Frank's complaint was well rehearsed, "Foxes, rats, the feathered fraternity." This last with heavy irony, "All of a sudden everybody's stuffing himself with my dinner."

"Least the badgers and the hedgehogs are still on the nod."

"Still not enough to go round, Max." The blackbird's legs were trembling now, his dark eyes filling. "Don't suppose you fancy a worm or two, though?"

The hopelessness of the question hung sadly between

them. Max looked down for a moment. "Better get this over with, Frank."

As he looked down, Max knew he'd pay for the regret. Frank thrashed his wings frantically, beating up a cloud of tiny particles of twiglet and leaf spine. Max shut his stinging eyes and pulled back to strike blind at where he thought the blackbird was. But as he launched himself through the air, he could hear Frank crashing through where the terrified thrush had already opened a hole in the twig curtains.

By the time Max had his eyes opened and his nose out of the hedge, the blackbird was perched in a baby hawthorn in the hedgerow across the lane. It pulled a few feathers back into shape.

"In a way, I'm happy it went like this," Frank called down breathlessly from the top of the shrub, "and in another way," he drew himself up and spat out at the top of his voice, "beak you, you mud-scuffling gut-reeking flesh-shredder!"

Max pulled his head back in. You never know when there's a sparrowhawk about. Until it's too late. "Come on, Frank." It was a pained protest. "I'm a stoat. What do you expect?"

He looked down at his feet and then called out again. "Your worm's still here."

"Hungry I may be," replied the blackbird, "but imbecilic…" He flapped his wings, sent a satisfied dropping into the hedge beneath. "Still, if you hang around long enough, that thrush'll be back for it."

"You fight your own battles," Max called over, signalling the danger, at least from him, was over. He gulped down the disputed worm halves and then moved off towards the lay-by and the next option in a fast diminishing menu.

❧

There was a large coughing box pulled up in the lay-by, with humans inside peering out through the look-throughs. It looked hot inside and there was a furious amount of noise bouncing around in there. Human females, by the sound of it. And most of them were young.

Stan the sparrow was perched in food-swooping position on the rim of the rotting food box, poised to make off with any crumbs or food particles the humans were foolish enough to let through their grasp. If they ever came out into the cold, that is.

Humans were gratifyingly sloppy in their eating habits, according to Stan who made his living out of their cascading detritus. So he waited patiently for one of two of them to tumble out of the box as they nearly always did once they'd stopped.

He picked Max up without turning. "They got a dog in there with them. A little one. Wouldn't come out." he reported.

"How little?" asked Max, slipping into his burdock patch. He knew Stan was feeding him information to stave off any inquiries into his own availability on the menu tonight.

"Well, bigger than you, old mate," replied the sparrow, frizzing out his neck feathers and settling back down for the long wait, "but didn't seem to have much of a bite on it."

"Where's your mob?" Stan always had his family with him and Max didn't like anything out of the ordinary.

"Up the pigs," Stan shrugged. "Think it's a waste of time, meself. This lot are the ones that are holding."

A door opened at the front of the coughing box and a small dog was thrown out onto the gravel. It immediately tried to climb back in again but was met with a barrage of human female noise.

"Don't be such a baby, Georgie!"

Max tensed as he looked at Georgie. The dog had moved a few disconsolate steps towards the verge. Then it sat down and looked plaintively back over his shoulder at the human females back in the warm, all yelling at him through the look-through.

Georgie was a small spaniel with a tartan collar and thorns caught in his big floppy, furry ears. His sad brown eyes took some time to focus on Max in the deep shadows gathered around the burdock patch. But when he did, he blanched at the cold grey eyes, the razor teeth, the slanted ears and the bullet shaped stabbing skull.

"Just passing through," he mumbled, standing up and backing off a little. "You know how it is. No offence."

"Go on, Georgie!" came a muted yell of command. "You know you need to, you silly animal."

"The rabbits are underground," said Max, his stance frozen just pre-launch. "If you were after a run-around."

"I best get back." The spaniel glanced fretfully over its shoulder at the human females who appeared to be waving him away.

"They don't seem to want you in there," observed Max.

"My lot get nervy if I wander off," Georgie swallowed heavily after the obvious untruth. "Actually, they want me to… well, you know."

"And do you want to?"

"All the time, this weather," Georgie looked sadly at the ground, then, "but not right now, no."

"Best get back, then," agreed Max.

The spaniel turned forlornly back to coughing box. Then he started to bark. Loud barks, full of melancholy, which drifted off into a desperate echo. Finally the door opened and a female hand reached out to drag Georgie in by his collar, "Stupid dog!"

"Don't you dare ask me to stop before we get back to School!"

Max knew, however, that despite the anger in the human voices, Georgie's tail would be wagging. He could live with the disapproval. He could live with a bursting bladder. But he couldn't live with a glimpse of imminent death in the razor-toothed darkness that had suddenly fallen outside.

"That's me done for the day." The darkness had galvanised Stan and he took off to join his family in some out of the way roost. It was clearly too cold for any goodbyes.

Max sank back down in the burdock patch to review his options. He should have taken Frank, he knew, but that was past and the past never brought any food into the present. Or it hadn't so far.

And with the day birds all safely out of his and harm's way, that left just the fields and the wood. It was too cold for mice in the fields and that meant any owl working out there would pick him up amongst the stillness straightaway.

So, he had to forage the Oak Wood. It would be slightly warmer in the heart of it. Hopefully warm enough to encourage the bank voles and wood mice to wander that little bit further afield in the supposed safety of the new flower growth amongst the leaf mould.

Max cut back to the hedge that ran along the Roaring Road until the wheatfield joined the Oak Wood. A straight course along this and then a sudden jink up and across the stream and into the trees should take him safely into the killing ground.

It took only one small spasm from his stomach, reminding him of the lateness of the hour in an altogether hungry day, to prompt him into his first and hopefully last raiding probe of the night.

৪৯

It was as if it was some sort of signal. An eerie, coded announcement of some obscurely planned and inescapable ambush.

The moment Max moved through the treeline, a

dreadful wailing swirled out from the depths of the wood and encircled him. It was answered shortly from a direction further along the perimeter of the ancient trees by a baleful scream that extended beyond the possibilities of normal pain.

Max shook himself with exasperation. Foxes were on a mating run through the area. The reek by the human's burrow in the afternoon should have warned him. Now they were tracking each other through the shadowy tree trunks. There could be any number of vixens. Their noise just seemed to amplify out of any relation to their numbers and the males would run all night and all over the country to cover them.

Max stood up and raked the night with all his senses. The foxes would be too involved to worry about him. But if they kept up all this heart pounding activity they'd frightened most of the vole life back under ground, and flush all the mice out of his furthermost reach.

His main chance lay in killing as soon as possible, before the woodland had a real chance to register the fox orgy in its midst.

He had to make for the centre of the Oak Wood quickly now. He knew that, just past the bracken and the shrubs packed around the treeline, the woods swept into snowdrop covered banks as the size and age of the trees increased. So he sped under the hazel holding the wood line and then stole silently into the new flower growth as snowdrops and winter aconites spread across the forest floor.

Staying close under the snowdrop canopy, hoping to avoid any air attack and half hoping to meet a bank vole scampering the other way, Max kept up a steady pace towards the heart of the wood. Then for a moment the cover broke and he found himself crossing a narrow path that traversed the flower bank. He pulled up on the far side and scented intensely.

The first of the bad news had been the short grey hairs he'd nosed through on his way across. These hairs turned a forest path into a badger run. The rest of the bad news was the fresh, dense scent of the badger they belonged to. A scent that hung in a menacing fug all around him.

Fornicating foxes and a recently awakened badger. The wood couldn't get much more dangerous than that.

Max supposed it must be warmer than he thought. It would take something like that to pull the badger out of his torpor. Everybody with an interest in survival was aware that, unlike hedgehogs and dormice, badgers didn't really hibernate round here. Still you didn't expect to run into one much before early spring.

In fact the cold normally kept them out of the way until March, when their natural drives to mate, intimidate and murder drew them out from under to terrorise the neighbourhood.

Well, for all that, one was already out and about. An established male from the reek. But whether he was on the lookout for worms or mayhem was anybody's guess and Max didn't intend to find out.

He plunged back under the snowdrops and pressed on in the safety of the darkness till the bank fell steeply away from him and his momentum increased beyond his liking or his absolute control. In fact he was moving at quite a speed by the time the flower cover ran out again and he found himself pulling himself up a couple of feet out onto the moonlight woodland floor.

Exposed, he hunched down to get his vision re-orientated, registering fast that he was in a clearing encircled by established oak trees, with moulting patches of frost flattened grass and leaf mould stretched between them.

And there across the clearing, cleaning his murderous claws on an unresisting oak trunk, he registered Don, an adult male badger known for his quickfire temper even amongst this rampaging species. And while both Don and Max were both fully paid up members of what wildlife in the neighbourhood called the Blood and Guts Crew, a badger was out in a lethal league of its own.

Everything fled from a badger except, on vicious occasion, the demented dogs that humans brought in to attack them. But those dogs had been driven somehow insane, maddened beyond any thought of natural predation or survival. Anything with any sense, however, kept right out of a badger's way. And now Max found himself too close to one.

Somewhere behind Don a vixen shrieked out its lust and its driven desperation to conceive. But he paid no attention. Instead he spun round and scented, half-blindly, at Max.

"Stoat," he concluded. "Stoat on its own." Then he peered at Max, "You're living dangerously."

"It's Max, Don." There was an outside chance the personal touch might slow things down. It hadn't worked for him with Frank it was true. But on the badger's ground, picked out in the moonlight, he had to try everything.

A dog fox barked out its carnal intentions to the vixen and was answered by a rival which barked out a challenge for the mate neither of them had run down yet.

"Puts my teeth on edge. When they do that," Don spoke in a malignant whisper. "Ought to have some consideration."

"They're all over the forest."

"Won't last long round here." Don gave his sturdy ribs a furious scratch. "Not if they try all that yowling round me."

"You're out early, Don."

"That a problem?" his hackles rose, already a pretext for mayhem had registered and was building into his attack pattern.

"Just an observation." Max kept his tone as mild as it would go. He couldn't even retreat now without setting the onslaught in motion. "You're not usually about this time in the month. That's all."

"Want to know why I'm out and about, Max?" Don gave a cold laugh that would have passed for a cough in another species. "It's a joke. Really. Considering."

"Considering?"

"Considering the racket those shabby tail-chasers are making." Don's teeth bared in an enraged snarl as another dog fox howled out his credentials and Max felt his blood cool at the sight. The badger stared long and hard at him. Then considered another flea-raking, even going as far as to lift his rear leg. But the moment passed and he set it down again and shook himself instead. "I came out for a bit of peace," he explained.

"Wouldn't have thought it'd get lively down in your place."

"Five breeding females. Two of them birthing right now." Don wasn't looking at him any more. His focus was underground now, in the sett he'd taken weeks to build. "And the noise, Max, the noise. Thought I had it all set up. We'd built right out – set out some lovely rooms for 'em. Bit of privacy." His eyes narrowed at the word. "Privacy. Joke that turned out to be. I'm due a bit of privacy, right?"

"It's your sett, Don." Max started to back slowly away. "You should have pride of place."

"Try telling that to a bunch of mothers, all screeching and straining and thrashing about." The badger breathed deeply and shook his head at the thought. "Then there's all the mess to contend with and the endless grooming and shuffling about. And there's still one to pop and the others are all sniffy about the new litters and everybody's moving about too scratching early."

"So you come out for a bit of peace." Max could feel his hindquarters backing into the snowdrops.

"And now this lot are at it an' all." Don turned sharply, as a vixen called in her suitors. "World's gone sex mad."

"I'll leave you to it."

"Only come out for a few worms. Or a hedgehog, maybe. Don't know where there's a hedgehog going begging, do you?"

"Still all under, Don." Max's shoulders were under the canopy now, just his head held steady in case the ruminative badger should look up. This display of uncharacteristically maudlin self-pity could transform itself back into vengeful cruelty at any moment. "There might be a couple in the leaf banks back towards the stream, but there'll be none anywhere near your territory. You know that."

"I just need some sleep," said Don tersely.

"I know." Max ducked his head under the leaves.

"Right amount of sleep and I would've killed you the moment I saw you," said Don. "Now I can't be bothered."

The badger got up testily and padded off along his run deeper into the Oak Wood, away from the wailing foxes. And Max felt a little of what he thought Georgie must have felt when he got back into the coughing box full of young human females. Still in trouble but alive. Every inch of him, still alive. There seemed to be a pattern forming that night. Frank, Georgie, himself. All three of them alive when they shouldn't be.

He only hoped the pattern broke once he got near something he could kill and eat. Thinking about it, the foxes would be spreading shock waves throughout the wood's vole population. If he moved closer to the mating wails, he ought to come face to face with some rodent seeking a place of greater safety.

He stopped and listened acutely. After a minute or two the competing males howled out their claims and he fixed on the direction and set off towards them.

He was scenting ahead keenly and from time to time he would stop and, keeping his eyes shut so his hearing could work uncluttered, he'd listen for tiny panicking scuffles coming his way. The wood threw back many sounds from the shifting of twigs to the swaying of branches but no living sound came. He started forward a few paces and then froze to make doubly sure.

All at once a dizzying impact crashed down upon him, pounding him into the cold earth and knocking the breath from his body. A slicing agony followed, tearing along his shoulders and upper back as the air around him filled with feathers and muscle power.

The intense pain caused him to thrash sideways and

exert all his power to force himself over on his back. He slashed with his teeth at the fast gripping power above him and managed to jerk it to one side. Then, flailing with all four legs, he tried to push the weight away. He could feel his claws puncturing skin beneath the feathers and the grip loosened. In a fury built of pain and mortal fear, he threw himself into terrible and relentless mayhem till the opposing force abated and struggled free, to reshape itself into the form of a winded tawny owl inches away.

The owl staggered backwards and then took off for the safety of the sky. Max seized the opportunity and sprinted desperately for the sanctuary beneath the outstretched suckers of an ancient oak. Once there he sunk down to regain his breathing and his night awareness. Blood was flowing around his shoulders and the talon wounds gaped and ached.

"Max?" A soft female voice drifted over the night air above his ragged breathing.

"Evening Catherine." He couldn't show the pain. Nothing must give away his vulnerability.

Catherine was an adult tawny owl; no wonder he'd heard nothing. She must have seen him through the snowdrop canopy, which meant that there really couldn't be anything else moving about out there. He tried to turn his head back to check the extent of the damage. A spasm of pain shot through him and he gave out a cry of anger.

"You're hurt, aren't you, Max?" the owl called softly.

"Don't even think about it, Catherine." He backed further into the root cluster beneath the suckers. "Come down again, and I'll finish you off."

Catherine looked over both shoulders to see if anybody else was there to share the joke. "I don't think so, Max. I know you're badly cut up. You'll bleed to death by dawn."

"I'll see you then. Take a wing off, maybe."

Max tried to squeeze under the root cluster, to see if he could work his way round the tree and out of Catherine's night vision. No animal could outplay her at night, and few would escape by day.

He was dazed and he was wounded, how badly he could not tell, but he couldn't allow the shock to overcome him. She'd pick him off in seconds. However, there was no easy way round the oak. He'd just have to sit it out and will himself to stay alert and alive. If he got lucky, something else would bustle through the clearing that Catherine could take home to the nest. Preferably something sizeable.

He needed her away from the area for some time. After all, with his wounds, he didn't know if could run at all, let alone sprint back towards the wood's perimeter.

ॐ

"Max?"

Max forced his eyes to open wider and focus out onto the wood with all its bleak prospects. A long time had passed. The night was at its darkest and Catherine was still perched an infuriatingly short and safe distance away.

His whole body was stiff from the enfolding cold and the shock that pounded right down to the bones. He said nothing.

"Oh, come on, Max, I can see you breathing."

He shifted, trying to pull himself into the attack position and winced as pain shot through the numbing ache that filled him. His body felt like the dead dogs he had found on the Roaring Road, stiff, heavy and going nowhere. He pulled his head up to look for his nemesis.

"Legs not working?" Catherine cooed. "I'll be down soon. Take you out of the pain."

Another carnal scream rent the night. The foxes were still on their prowling. They'd been at it for hours. It had been one of the things that had kept Max awake and alive. If only he could feed off their stamina now.

Nothing had fled through the clearing; Catherine hadn't moved an inch. And if he didn't take her on now, the last of his strength would desert him. He'd be stuck trapped against the tree bole like an oversized, bleeding bank vole. It had to be now. He slumped and dropped his head heavily, hoping she'd pick it all up.

"It's not good, Catherine," he admitted, keeping his voice weak and breathless. "But I don't think it's as bad as…. Why don't you just come and find out?"

The owl fluffed her chest feathers, nibbled at one to tidy it away, "Everything in good time." She turned her huge eyes back down to Max. "You're a fair amount of meat, Max. Worth waiting for."

He kept his head down, hoping she was assured enough to make a surprise crash dive. The seconds passed like days. Then without any forewarning a fox was screaming in the shrub feet away to his right.

He pulled his head up to see something small and furry scampering out of the shrub and hurling itself headlong across the clearing. He saw the blur of feathers that met it half way, heard its piercing shriek and knew Catherine hadn't been able to resist her instincts.

The instant the owl delivered the death bite and registered her mistake, Max was already on the move. He sprung over the root cluster and ran through the oak suckers, through the crocus shoots that fringed them, through the pain that twisted across him and into the snowdrop banks.

His muscles were howling in agony, his heart was pounding, his eyes blinded by cold and blood and his lungs were screaming for air. But he built up the pace. He needed to find a burrow, a safe haven somewhere on the wood's edge where he could take stock. He had to gather himself sufficiently to snatch enough food to be able lie up and lick his wounds. A burrow nearer the Roaring Road was his only chance, and a slim one at that.

Behind him the foxes moaned their way towards each other, and Catherine flew back to her nest with a dead wood mouse and a lot more work to do before dawn.

As the noises receded, he slowed to a less painful pace and loped into the scrub that fringed the forest where it joined the world of the Roaring Road. He could pick up the sounds of the stream by the humans' wall that stretched up to the duckpond and held back the wheatfield. Even the sounds were calmer here.

He veered off through the bracken and the bramble at the wood's outermost reaches, towards the sound of the stream. Generations of voles and mice had burrowed around there. This time of year it was both energy consuming and frustrating trying to flush out the winter survivors, but there were labyrinths of abandoned homes. And right now he needed to be underground even more than he needed to eat.

In his weakened state, he didn't find it as much as stumble into it. It was small, overgrown but welcoming enough to trip him up and draw him in. A neglected rodent nest burrowed into a scrubby bank that tilted awkwardly into the bushes leading down to the stream.

He squeezed his way into it, scraping his flayed back on its crumbling roof, nosing his way gratefully into its tiny central chamber in which he lay, filling it as his pounding lungs expanded. He drank in the darkness, the stillness, and the close safeness of it all and closed his eyes.

Max monitored his heartbeat and his breathing as they steadied but still something wasn't quite right. The breathing he heard didn't quite match the breathing he felt in his now relaxing body.

He opened his eyes and saw, inches away, the quivering whiskers of the unluckiest bank vole in the country.

ৡৡ

It was a bright morning when, rested and fed, Max eased his way into the daylight. The foxes were long gone, sleeping it off somewhere either happily exhausted or morosely dissatisfied. Don would have elbowed his way to a grumpy pride of place in his secret sett and Catherine, well he hoped she'd starved but knew she hadn't.

Two blue tits were pairing off, leapfrogging after each other in a bush beside him. Further away some yellowhammers were flitting along the hedgerow top, singing out as they flicked their tails nervously. The wood felt like a different place in the morning sunshine.

There was still any number of threats waiting to spring out on him but the cool air on his back, and the loosening of his shoulders gave him a surge of confidence. So he stalked purposefully back into the bracken to see what might be moving about on the wood's perimeter. He didn't feel ready for the heart of it yet, and the scent of dead bank vole would have cleared the immediate area of any morning snack.

"Here we go, here we go," said a sharp harsh voice. "Should be just round here. Somewhere."

"You sure, Barry?" answered something similar.

Max eased his head through some scrubby bracken just as the male jay hopped awkwardly towards him. But it was staring at a patch in the ground some feet before him.

"Elaine," he called exasperatedly over his shoulder. "I know what I'm doing."

Elaine, his long-term mate, hopped in ungainly circles a few feet away. She paused and fidgeted. "Sorry," she called over but it didn't sound as if she meant it.

"There you go," Barry said triumphantly as he unearthed a long stashed acorn, crushed and swallowed it.

"Thanks," replied Elaine, miffed. "Thanks a bunch."

But Barry had turned and was hopping erratically over towards some hawthorn. "Now there's two more over here I put down during the last big icy."

"Well, leave one for me," she called after him and then spotting Max's head in the bushes, she fired out a harsh warning note. "Max is in the bracken."

The male jay looked over at him and sized him up carefully. "Flap me, Max. You look like something ate you."

"Ate him and spat him out," agreed Elaine.

"Bit of owl trouble," said Max. He'd never get near them today. Jays were a tough call at the best of times. Beautifully marked, they were awkward on the ground, clumsy in the air and restless on the branch. But their big brown-pink bodies were deceptively fast.

"Catherine was out late," observed Elaine. "We heard her finishing off as we came out."

"You never got tucked up by Catherine?" Barry snorted, highly amused. "Blood and Guts Boy like you."

"It can get you any time, Barry," said Max coldly. "You know that."

Barry stood hesitantly by the hawthorn. He looked to Elaine and then over to Max and then slowly flapped his wings. He looked a little awkward.

"I'm not after your acorns," said Max shortly. "Look at me. Do I look like someone in crying need of your acorns?"

"No. Right. OK." That bit of business concluded to his satisfaction, Barry dug out another stash. Elaine hopped across to him and the two big, colourful birds crunched away on them.

"Maybe you'd just leave the mice and the eggs to me," Max suggested with just a hint of acid. He knew there wasn't a chance.

"No problem," Mumbled Barry generously, his beak full of pulped nut.

"Lovely day," Elaine completed the civilities before getting her beak back down to makes sure her partner didn't finish the hoard. This was a matter of principal rather than practicality. They had other pantries buried throughout the Oak Wood and they never forgot the sites.

Max looked up at the clear blue sky. "Could well be, couldn't it?"

And he turned back in the direction of the lay-by to see if something unwary might be sniffing its way round the rotting food box. A little breakfast, a long day's sleep and some careful cosseting of the clotted gashes on his back and tonight who knows, he might be right back on his old form.

Barry and Elaine watched him go. Bloodied and ragged but steady and soft footed as he blended into the hazel.

"Nobody gets away from an owl." Elaine shook her head in quiet amazement. "Catherine must be pecking herself."

"I'll peck her if I ever catch up with her." Barry stabbed at an acorn that had rolled beyond him. Then looked up to catch a last glimpse of Max's battle-scarred form as it disappeared from safe view. "Just think of the trouble she's left us with."

# March

## Apocalypse Pond

The birds were giving nobody any peace, least of all each other. Their incessant clamour swirled and surged with no apparent pattern, like the winds which gusted through the day in erratic squalls, bringing with them unsettling bursts of driving, stinging rain.

In the woods the redwings chattered, the chaffinches yelled and shrieked and the green finches squealed and buzzed. Even some early chiff-chaffs had turned up, clinking away about their time in the southern sun. The wrens bellowing in the treetops capped them all, however; you could hear them clear across the country. The great spotted woodpeckers were hammering at the oaks warning off all the other woodpeckers in the area. Even the sparrowhawks had broken their habitual silence and were making their shrill lamenting and annual contribution to the grand cacophony.

Out in the fields, the lapwings tumbled and called, the little owls yelped, and the kestrels made their presence felt at altitude.

Further over by the pond, the coots were sniping at each other while the mallards pompously disputed property rights to the stream that fed into it. Canada geese were honking at some passing shelduck who were returning in kind.

In the lay-by, Frank the blackbird landed on the rim of the rotting food box and tilted his head to listen to the general exchange. Then he threw his head back and opened his throat.

"Don't you start," snapped Max, as he rested in his burdock patch. And Frank almost lost his footing. "What is wrong with you lot?"

"Just keeping in touch," observed Frank. "It's a healthy occupation, Max. You ought to try it."

"Load of empty noise."

"Not really. It's all about nesting and mating and warning off the opposition," Frank explained. "Don't you like mating, Max?"

"I don't go bawling about it from the tops of trees," replied Max.

"Fastest way to find one," smiled Frank.

"Fastest way to pull a sparrowhawk down on you."

"There is that," conceded the blackbird, "but most of us feel mating's worth the risk." Then he cocked an eye at the stoat. "Watch this."

Frank pushed his chest out and opened his beak and immediately, Max could hear him calling "Biggest blackbird in the area! Come and get him, ladies!"

His voice dominated the general bird noise but, more interestingly, it seemed to be coming from the hawthorn bush at the end of the lay-by. Max looked from the bush to Frank and back again.

"Little trick," said Frank with quiet pride. "That way you can see who's turning up to look for you."

"That's quite something, Frank."

"If it's a female, you fly over. If it's a hawk, you just don't turn up."

"What happens if a female and a hawk show at the same time."

"Love can be cruel sometimes," smiled Frank. Then he looked down the road and for some reason his good spirits seemed to leave him. He shifted his weight from foot to foot and looked unhappy and uncomfortable.

Max followed his eye line to see Brian and Ray, the crow brothers, land heavily at the far end of the lay-by and walk across with their purposeful rolling gait. Small wonder Frank had turned in on himself. Nobody liked to give the crows an excuse for an explosion of mayhem.

Brian arrived first. He looked hard at Frank, but talked to Max. Brian liked to hold unsettling conversations. "Don't suppose you're much interested in toads, Max?" he said.

"Toads? What about toads?"

"Road's jumping with them." Ray put an extra burst of speed into his saunter to catch up with his brother and deliver the news. "Fact they're all over the road. Dead and alive."

"Back up in the Oak Wood," Brian filled in. "They're on their run through to the pond."

"Toad time again." Frank looked thoughtful.

"Stuffed full of them, I am," Ray remarked aggressively. "They got no idea what the Roaring Road's for."

"Maybe it's for giving you a squashed toad dinner, Ray," Frank suggested. And he edged himself round to the safer side of the rotting food box rim.

"And the rest."

Max thought about this, "Place'll be jumping with frogs then. If the toads are on the move."

"Won't be any room left for water. In that pond," Brian pronounced. He cocked his head up and held it still before looking around irritably, "Noisy round here isn't it?"

You're a bird, thought Max, you should be used to all this. But he said nothing. He wanted Brian and Ray to move on. Not hang around, holding him up with their roadside bravado.

"Cats. Rabbits. Hedgehogs. Foxes," Ray chanted out his diet at Frank. "All squashed. Lovely."

"Going to get busy up there, Brian, that's for sure," agreed Max. The more he thought about it, the more the toad and frog spawning made the pond sound like the place to be. You could make a good meal of frogs' legs if you ate enough of them and the spawning would be stirring up half the neighbourhood. And a stirred up neighbourhood meant confused mice and voles scurrying about. Something to add to the menu.

"We got more'n we can handle up the road," said Brian affably. "Just thought we'd drop down and pass you the good word."

Max's suspicions hardened. The crows did very little for each other and nothing for anyone else. Except once in a while they would throw some grand, magnanimous gesture like letting a lost duckling go free, just to prove to the world they had a warm, sentimental side despite appearances.

"All heart. That's me," Brian added dryly, but he left the challenge dangling between them. He looked off to one side, daring one of them to deny his better nature, so the usual crow protocol of loudly proclaimed grievance followed by inevitable and murderous violence could begin.

"All heart," agreed Frank, mechanically.

"Thanks for the nod, Brian." Max went through the motions too.

"Heart. Guts. Lungs. Lot to be had out of toad," advised Ray, "long as it's not too spread out."

The sun forced its way through the cloud cover and the wheatfield behind them lit up. The moment seemed ripe and Max moved off instantly towards the perimeter hedge. His sudden start caused Brian to jump backwards in alarm with awkward, off balanced wingbeats. Frank, sensing an attack, flew directly to the top of the hawthorn, calling stridently while Ray cawed savagely as he wheeled round on the world at large.

Max paused by the hedge, stood up and chattered, "I'll give it the once over, then, Brian."

The elder crow pulled his back straight and cocked his massive head at the stoat. "Mind how you go, Max," he spoke with an icy fury at the temporary loss of his dignity. "It's a dangerous world out there."

But Max had moved through the hedge and was loping through the field towards the duckpond. He moved at speed over the ploughed ground, highly attuned to the likelihood of a sudden tearing attack from the skies. His back was only just healing from Catherine the owl's talons and the soreness served as a continuous warning, a throbbing part of his air defences.

He was checking the clearing skies when the sound of raised voices ahead pulled him up sharply, and he crept behind a churned up earth mound to investigate.

"You're out of your mind, Bradshaw!" The voice was strained and ended in a high pitched mocking laugh. "Nothing but a leaping, frothing loony!"

"You'd know of course, Ripley!" came the outraged retort.

"You're madder than your mother, and she was a real dribbler!"

"Leave my mother out of this!" The first voice was beside itself.

"Gladly. Wouldn't share the same field with a demented old Jill like that. Wouldn't be healthy. Might rub off." The second voice wavered as it rose. The owner was clearly a little unstable himself.

Max pushed his head round the earth mound to see two full grown male hares standing up to each other in a small dip amid the furrows. They seemed to sense the movement and looked round wildly.

"Who's that?" screamed Ripley.

"Keep your voice down," hissed Bradshaw as he settled back on all fours. "Could be foxes."

"Could be anything," Ripley sounded haunted.

"Creeping in," Bradshaw echoed him.

"With murderous intent." And suddenly Ripley shouted, "Get away from us! We're big and fast and we fight to the death."

Bradshaw leapt back onto his hind legs and flourished his forepaws, "Don't bring 'em over here, you maniac! Shut up or I'll box your ears!"

"Fancy your chances, do you?" Ripley leapt to his hind legs too and squared up. There was a flurry of blows.

Max edged round the churned up mound. These hares were too big to take and life in an exposed field, coupled with the need to mate in it, had clearly taken their toll on the animals' frame of mind. Max knew hares to be unhinged at best and potentially lethal on occasion. He'd taken leverets before, of course, but that was different. Young never normally posed any problems, once they were separated from any family grouping. But these boys were deranged and best left to their own unbalanced devices.

So he set off to outflank them, unseen, and had gone a few feet down a particularly handy furrow when he entered a sharpish turn and came face to face with a female stoat. They both froze and stared at each other.

She was young and healthy with shining eyes. She met his gaze steadily and then shifted her own to look over his shoulder in a silent indication that he was in her way. When her gaze finally returned to his, he held her attention through a subtle redistribution of weight and the raising of his shoulders in preparation for... what? She waited for him to make his intentions clear.

A few feet away they could hear the drumming of feet and the pounding of forepaws as the hares' continued their bout. And then as suddenly as it had started, it stopped.

Max widened his eyes fractionally, acknowledging to her that he had registered the silence. Until a cracked voice came in over the furrows.

"I tell you there's something there, you lunatic!"

"Stoats! I can smell stoats."

"Always a drama. Couldn't be just one stoat, could it? Oh no! Has to be a pack of the little bastards!"

Max pressed his mouth to her ear to introduce himself. "I'm Max. Centred on the lay-by."

"Claire," she was polite but nothing more. "I need to go that way."

Once again the sound of punches being exchanged, interspersed by sudden dramatic flying kicks, blasted through the afternoon's convoluted birdsong. Max nodded to Claire and leaned to one side of the furrow to let her pass. She pressed past him to continue on her way and as she moved through he scented at her rear, to set her properly in his memory.

Feeling his whiskers upon her, she turned and looked haughtily back. "It's the wrong time and you're the wrong stoat."

"Fine." Max tried to sound unaffected by this. "Managed to trap the right one have you?"

"I'm carrying for Big Dave." She made a little mocking grimace at him after she'd said it. "Littering in weeks."

"Congratulations." He could wait. "See you later."

She looked evenly at him, weighing him up from the sheen on his fur to the healing scrapes on his back and then, "Go play with the hares."

She moved off stealthily and with a fluid grace but Max could see that her sleek body was beginning to thicken slightly at the rear. She was carrying all right. Another litter for Big Dave.

As an established male, Big Dave would have households across the country. He mated with the youngest, healthiest, choicest females. And these females would carry his seed all year round, staying trim enough for burrow hunting before breaking off in spring, the time of plenty, to gestate and bear the litter.

In this way, Big Dave controlled a year's worth of social life in the local stoat population. And one day Max would have to make a move on him. If life itself didn't take care of the problem. Still, Claire had definitely shown some interest. He wouldn't always be the wrong stoat at the wrong time. Probably.

In the meantime he had frogs' legs to eat.

He reached the far side of the field without further incident and slid into the hedge that ran between it and the lane. Across from him the humans' green patch fell away towards some alders, two old willows and the tussock sedges that flanked the nearest end of the pond itself.

At the pond's edge, reeds and rushes jostled with crowfoot, plantains and marestail and through it all hopped a multitude of aroused frogs. Both sexes, in all shapes and sizes. All calling out the obvious with deep dedication and increasing urgency.

"Frog here!"

"Big frog here!"

"Frog coming!"

They palpated in the coarse grass on their way to the plant cover and the shallow water that promised to be the site of their annual consummation. They jumped and croaked, or stood still and announced their presence before jumping on to see what connections were to be made. And their low voiced calling may have hugged the grass but at ground level it overwhelmed the bird noise with its rhythmic insistence.

"Bigger frog here!"

"Coming! Coming!"

At the nearest end of the pond was a muddy slipway, flanked with sedge. If he set himself right in the plant cover there, his food would simply leap towards him. He knew he wouldn't be the only animal taking advantage of the amphibians' mating instincts. But if any other predator turned up to make a nuisance of himself, he'd simply fade away in the tangle of bramble and nettles on the far side. Once in there, he had all manner of escape routes back across the lane and into the wheatfield.

He scanned the green patch for humans but apart from an old female standing alone in the field of tall stones beside the pointed burrow, way off, the whole arena seemed empty. This was odd, considering the number of burrows clustered around the green patch and the number of coughing boxes still and silent before them.

Clearly the humans had no interest in the steady stream of frogs and toads arriving in their midst. But humans were like that. Wasteful. You only had to look at the food they scattered around them to know that.

He crossed the lane rapidly and made for the sedge, ignoring the frogs bouncing along in the same direction. He'd have plenty of time to scoop them up later, when away from prying, human eyes.

"Frog here!"

"Frog coming!"

He settled into the secure bulk of the tussock and took stock of the frog extravaganza. The bank was covered in young males all calling out their mating credentials while the females jumped over to them. The males with the deepest voices seemed the most popular, regardless of size. Their croak was their virility.

The shallows were boiling with unattached males grasping at whatever approached. Couples tumbled in around them, to add to the confusion, the males kicking and grunting, the females bulging and distended.

Mating couples slowly traversed the water in an amorous clamping that would end in a languorous spawning and swift parting, hours or maybe even days later. As their eyes bulged and their feet clutched, they filled the shallows with frogs' eggs. The jellified result of a job well done.

Of course the whole neighbourhood fell on them. From his vantage point, Max could see Harry the hedgehog and his angry son Cliff lurking in some marestail, snaffling up the happy couples and munching them conscientiously with small huffles of pleasure.

The other frogs didn't seem to notice or mind. They were there to breed, not outrun hedgehogs. They didn't notice the grass snakes either or the heron standing motionless in the shallows as they swam out to discharge their parental obligations.

There were so many frogs that the heron didn't bother to stretch for the further flung prospects, but waited to strike at those within easy reach. It swallowed a frog whole whereas the hedgehogs chewed away stolidly and the grass snakes used their lengthy and secretive procedures. The poisonous sacs within the frogs' torsos didn't seem to affect them. But sometimes it was like that. One animal could eat something that would kill the next.

Max would just eat the legs. So that meant he needed a lot of frogs.

He got to work. Pulling a frog to him, he bit off the legs and tossed the rest away. The front half of the frog kept moving towards the water before expiring as he flopped into it. Max took another and another and a small pile of shuddering bodies built up around him, so he moved along the pondside before the remains signalled his presence.

Cliff the hedgehog, however, picked him up almost immediately. "Wasting a lot there, Max!" he called over crossly while his father, Harry, chomped his way through a large fat female.

"Once I move on," Max bit into the next amorous couple, "you can help yourself."

"Think we'll manage." Cliff scuttled out for a frog whose bright green colouration particularly attracted him. "Toads is further round. If that's your fancy."

"I was wondering," Max confessed, "but I'm not really bothered."

He saw the flash of dirty red fur slinking up in the brambles, and debated whether to alert Cliff or not. Then, reasoning that any kind of trouble here involving the hedgehog would bring the feeding to a standstill, he did the decent thing.

"Foxes, Cliff," he warned.

Cliff sped back into the marestail. He and Harry pulled a couple of frogs into the heart of the plants with them and hunkered down. Seconds later a big dog fox arrived at the water's edge with a young vixen in tow.

They sniffed around busily.

The heron took off and flew in a lazy circle before returning to a motionless stand on the far side of the pond. On this day of plenty a couple of foxes weren't going to scare her away. So she waited patiently as the flotilla of waterborne lovers floated inexorably her way.

Back in the foxes' earth, the older vixens would be in labour and the dog fox would soon be starting up his supply runs. He'd be feeding the sucklers for weeks, while the barren vixens did a little babysitting and lay around hoping that things might be different the next season. He snapped up a frog greedily and then darted after another. The young vixen stood undecided behind them.

"Look at 'em all, Phil," she said breathlessly.

"Don't look, Dawn, eat. They won't be around for ever."

"What they all doing here, then?" she said, dutifully throwing a frog up, wolfing it back and then nosing another.

"Their big day, Dawn." He discovered a frog jam in a muddy cleft beside an alder and gobbled at it. "They're making babies."

"Kind of a way is that to behave? There's crowds of them."

"Just be barking thankful." Phil cleaned up Max's heap of the legless, without seeming to notice the discrepancy. He was feeding himself up for paternity.

Max sprinted away to a bramble patch off the slipway and just beside the older willow and threw himself into it. The frog traffic was lighter here but he hoped that any rodent life, not already disturbed by the crowds, might be flushed this way by the heady scent of Phil and Dawn.

He knew Cliff and Harry would lie low until the foxes tired of that particular stretch of pondside or were spooked by some passing human and moved off. So he crouched by the water where the bramble had snared some tatty reeds and watched the foxes snapping inexpertly at the jumping frogs.

Then suddenly something moved in the bramble right behind him.

Instinctively, Max had turned and slashed out with his teeth before he could identify the intruder. It slithered out of his bite leaving a taste so revolting that he found himself arch-backed and vomiting out partially digested frogs' legs. He focussed desperately through the tears to discover a large adult toad lying on its back beside him, wincing and palpitating wildly.

"Ted?" he coughed between mouthfuls of regurgitating frog. "That you?"

Ted the toad flopped himself onto his front and then leapt over to the waterside. He seemed intact but his bulging eyes scanned the world around him before returning to Max, and fixing him with a stony stare. "I hope you spew your tail, you meddling cretin."

"Didn't know it was you, Ted. Could've been a fox." The nausea came in waves, racking him, and the toad's implacable stare was making him very angry. Only it was difficult to sustain any fury with a stomach that kept trying to leave his body.

"Do I look like a fox?"

Max managed to gather himself. He breathed in deeply, trying to bring his insides to order. "Didn't see," he panted himself to a standstill then nodded towards the water. "Shouldn't you be in there mating?"

"Got a system. One of the reasons I'm still here."

Max felt emptied, but his clarity of thought had been returned to him. "Hanging back, then?"

The toad's eyes swivelled out to the slow procession of toads making their way down to the water on the far side of the willow. "I let the young bloods get in there first. Make all the noise. Draw the foxes and the buzzards and the hedgehogs. Time I turn up the girls are panting for it. And there's more chance of getting out to do it next year."

Max groomed the frog mess from his fur, "System's got a few faults though, hasn't it Ted?"

"Still here. Bit chewed but still here." Ted looked out at the deep water at the pond's centre. The toads were converging on it while the frogs, keeping to the shallows,

drew the attention of the heron. He fixed Max with a glinting stare again. "Never plan for sheer incompetence, can you?"

Max grimaced. Whether it was a spasm of nausea or a gripe of chagrin, he was not about to tell the toad. He had known Ted longer than Frank the blackbird. They too had always gone their separate ways, and now the relationship had changed. One had tried and failed to eat the other.

"Fox coming," observed the toad and Max swivelled round to organise his next defensive response.

He needn't have bothered. Dawn had splashed straight into the shallows to snap up a large female toad making stately progress out to the good time waiting for her in deeper waters. The young vixen turned in triumph towards Phil who was standing back on the slipway looking on with a curious grin as she bit through the toad with relish.

She spat it out almost immediately and retched loudly, standing splay legged in the water. Phil snapped up a frog that jumped past him and chewed contentedly before remarking, "Not a good move, love. Taste horrible, toads."

The vixen had obviously taken in quite a lot of toad and was spraying as much as she could on the water around her.

"Why don't you Blood and Guts lot ever learn?" Ted said sadly. "I could have mated with her. Bit big. But healthy."

"It's disgusting!" Dawn shrieked between spasms. "Not going to kill me is it, Phil?"

"Stick to frogs, you might survive. Long as anything as daft as you can survive."

Dawn waded disconsolately out of the pond and stood shivering and bedraggled before him. Phil sniffed at her and then turned back towards the frogs thronging the slipway.

"I don't think I can face any more," whined the vixen.

"They'll take the taste away," the dog fox smiled, "after a while."

The water was full of amphibians creating new life. While the shore was filling up with others waiting to devour it. Then, without warning, two human young ran down the slipway. And this time Max found Dawn and Phil really were streaking towards his cover.

"Euueh" the first human young, a female, made a sick noise as she looked around the slipway. "They're everywhere!"

"Get your jar out," shouted the young human male as he knelt by the water with a look-through thing that he dipped in the water. "We'll need loads and loads of eggs."

"Will they all be tadpoles?"

"We had lots at school last year. They grew legs and everything. Didn't they, Mum?"

Dawn and Phil crashed over the top of Ted and Max with scarcely a downward glance. They darted into the thicker bramble and set off circling their way back to the lane. At the rate they were going, they'd be back in the wheatfield in a few seconds. Dawn and Phil had no time for adult humans. And they'd picked up the arrival of the adult human female earlier than Max. This female had joined the young one, so now humans were taking up most of the useful feeding area on the slipway itself.

"Look at the toads over that way!" The adult human pointed. "See? The heron's going for them."

"Shoo!" shouted the young female but the heron didn't appear to be listening. She was too busy feeding.

Ted watched the foxes disappear and then turned towards the water. "I think it's time I widened my social circle."

"Isn't that heron going to be a problem?"

"Plenty of pond for the two of us," said Ted, "but the better looking females are being snapped up. Chiefly by her."

"And you don't want an ugly one, do you?"

"I'm too old to make do, Max." Ted plopped into the water and swam off in strong, stealthy strokes to make the most of his ageing social graces.

Max watched Ted making steady headway for a while, and then he turned and ducked under the willow tree where he could fall upon stragglers and lost lovers. Under the drooping branches and out of sight of the humans on the slipway, little piles of frog bodies built up across the ground.

It was easy work, but the flavour of frog seemed to contain an echo of the appalling flavour of toad and he was growing weary of it. In fact it was beginning to irritate him.

The foxes would be in the field by now and that would cause pandemonium amongst the rodents there. Even now, it was a fair bet rabbits would be scurrying for the tussocks on the field's boundaries. Certainly field mice and voles would be sneaking away from them, probably intending to sidle off down the hedge by the lane back to the Roaring Road. That's the escape route he'd have planned.

Rabbits of course never planned anything. Except for more rabbits.

Still, pandemonium there would be. Nothing like a fox for stirring things up. Unless it was a badger and he couldn't operate around a badger. He'd be one of the animals racing to keep out of the way. With foxes though it was an entirely different manner. So it was definitely worth taking a look down that lane beside the field. As soon as the humans moved off, he made up his mind to cross back to it and make a leisurely foray around the hedge and back to the Roaring Road.

His frog killing rate had slowed now as the flavour of vole called to him. After all, most of the work would be done for him. The foxes would make their presence felt in the field and he, Max, would tidy up the repercussions. Provided he could get over to them in safety.

He stood up to check how the humans were getting on. They were of course the biggest threat in the area but they seemed quite happy pottering about on the slipway, which no doubt was driving Cliff the hedgehog into a mute and hungry fury. Max shrugged and stayed put, loading up on frogs legs and tossing the torsos on the heap.

Humans moved at their own, incomprehensible pace; he had plenty of time after all.

Ripley stood on his own in the field. He gave a few feints with his paws and then sat down and sniffed. Almost at once he was up again. "You can't talk like that to me!" he yelled, eyes burning with anger.

He punched viciously at the air. Then leapt and delivered a lethal aerial kick behind him. "Who do you think you are?"

The only answer was the continuing bird noise but Ripley didn't seem to hear that. He stood tall. He dragged air in through his wildly dilated nostrils. He raked the empty field around him with murderous eyes. And then he sat down in his dip and gave a small shudder.

"Bradshaw?" he whispered in a quavering voice.

Phil and Dawn were approaching Ripley from opposite directions. That way, if the hare bolted, one fox could try and head it off into the other's attack. Surprisingly it didn't look as if this manoeuvre had been necessary. They were almost upon the animal and he hadn't made a single evasive move or shown the least awareness of the threat they posed. He just crouched low on the ground and from time to time a shiver ran through him.

Ripley didn't look. He didn't stand. After a while he just sighed and called softly over his shoulder in a shaky whisper, "Bradshaw, is that you?"

Dawn attacked with particular ferocity even for a vixen. She hadn't forgiven the toad for tasting so disgusting. Phil let her do most of the butchery and then settled down beside her for the feast.

And the birds sang on.

# April

## The Baby Boom

The elms and the sycamores were joining the chestnuts, the larches and the oaks in leaf. Forsythia was tangling itself in the hawthorn hedge and buttercups were opening in the meadows. And the rain beat down upon them all, sparkling in the morning sun.

The cuckoo was back and reminding everybody incessantly across the fields. And all the other birds were nesting. The wrens had given up their racket and taken to building. The males pulled up grass and new leaves to make any number of domed living options for the love of their life to choose to roost in. Each of them started several families and, after all the effort, Max reckoned they deserved it. And all the noise and fuss that went with it.

Over by the human green patch the wood pigeons, never too bright in his opinion, were feeding amongst the cherry blossom and often falling through the spindly twigs. They never seemed to fall far enough, though, and it was a waste of time waiting for one to hit the grass beneath. They never dropped an egg either.

Frank the blackbird was up beside his mate, whose tail and beak just protruded above the tall walls of the nest across the Roaring Road. She sat on their eggs with smug determination whilst Frank danced his obligatory attendance. He hardly had time to stop by at the lay-by and complain any more.

At least it was quieter.

Max sat in his burdock patch and watched the coughing boxes hissing past in the downpour. Very few pulled into the lay-by in the rain and when they did the humans very rarely got out. He'd noticed they didn't like to move about in the rain and supposed that, having no fur or feathers, their pink skin must be highly sensitive to it. Although the pigs in the pig fields didn't seem to mind and their skins looked very similar.

So the rotting food box remained empty, and the mice and sparrows had to search further afield for something to eat and that meant so would he. Once the rain had passed over he'd follow the verge along past the wheatfield and steal into the hayfield beside it and see if the rabbits had let their babies out to feed.

It was the time of the baby boom. Well the rabbits had been producing for weeks now, but so was everyone else. Eggs in nests. Babies in warrens. Litters in burrows. His countryside was filled with young or with the promise of young on the way. Even the badger cubs were out, although it would be a demented animal indeed that tried to take one of them.

It would be safer to snatch one of the tiny human young, Max thought as a small joke to himself. The humans were slower than an avenging adult badger and nowhere near as remorseless. Although from their sweet and sour smell he didn't expect them to taste very pleasant. Lot of meat on the bones though.

Back to the rabbits then. These were obligingly

produced in constant supply in the warrens on the far side of the stream by the Oak Wood, tucked away in the wild corner of the hayfield beside the lane leading up to the duckpond. He'd take the hayfield first and keep an eye out for a meadow nest filled with eggs on the way.

He checked the skies over the Pig Killers' from where the rain was drifting. Bright sunlight was glistening on the clouds there. So only a few more minutes of heavy rainfall and then he'd be off. The rain had beaten its way through the burdock and he was now getting drenched and the water was puddling at his feet.

Frank the blackbird flew over with a sharp aerial warning cry but simply couldn't resist it and landed in the top of the hawthorn. He gave a sturdy flap of the wings to shake off some rainwater and called down. "Part fish, are you?"

Max looked up at him with some irritation, "You're not making sense again, Frank."

"Just thinking. If you'd been born bright enough to build a nest, you wouldn't have to learn how to swim."

"Wouldn't get me stuck up a tree. Stuffing some eggbound female too lazy to get up and feed herself." Max had watched Frank's activities over the last few days. The blackbird had his work cut out and was getting little or no thanks, or even conversation, from his incubating mate. From what he knew of Frank, that would rankle.

"Joys of fatherhood, Max." Frank started off well enough but Max knew he wouldn't be able to sustain it.

"You ever get to sit in the nest yourself?" he held the taunt back under a note of sympathetic enquiry but Frank bridled anyway.

"Friendly concern is it? From the Blood and Guts Crew? You'll be eating dandelions next." He shook a raindrop off his beak with a contemptuous toss of his head but still took up the irresistible invitation to grumble. "Mind you, they don't half eat when they're brooding. Don't understand it. They don't go anywhere. They don't do anything. To use up that amount of fuel. Apart from the complaining. They do a lot of complaining."

"Joys of fatherhood, eh?" Max could see the rain thinning as the shower was sputtering out. "Best nip off for another worm. She'll fade away otherwise."

"Beak off, Max." He repositioned a wing feather and then gave a fatalistic shrug and one of his sideways looks. "You'll get it one day."

"Underground. In the warm. And then you leave 'em to it," smiled Max. "Nothing easier."

"You're all heart," replied Frank.

"You're all wet," said Max. "She won't like you dripping on the egglets."

Frank said nothing. He just looked thunderous and flapped off to find the next family worm. He knew that Max was right about dripping rainwater on the nest but he wasn't going to give him the satisfaction.

Max watched him fly off into the last of the rain and blinked as the sunlight burned through the hazy grey clouds and glittered in the puddles. Frank would find plenty of worms as the water bubbled back up from underground.

That brought him back to the rabbits. Now the rain had let up, the rabbits might poke their young out from the warrens and into the sunshine for a few fresh grass shoots. Even if only for a few well guarded moments.

He wouldn't need long.

He shook himself as much to loosen up his muscles as to throw off his personal coating of April rain and then sprinted up through the new yellow ragwort to the hedge where the wheatfield joined the Roaring Road.

The sun flooded out as he ran easily between the hedge and the nettle patches springing up along the verge. Often the nettles would provide a form of protection for frogs and the like but today they just provided him with cover. Which was enough to be going on with. He had rabbit on his mind.

He watched the hedge become reinforced with bits of old dark shiny and slats of rotted wood and knew, without peering through, that he was approaching the hayfield laid out in the space between the wheatfield and the lane leading up to the duckpond and the human burrows.

It was a strange area, this field, and it had a strange history. Ancient courses of contradictory furrows spread all over it, although you had to run them to know they were there, and there were all manner of plants growing side by side. In some parts the soil would stay rich and fertile, in others dried up and criss-crossed underground with long dead root systems. The humans didn't control it the way they controlled the wheatfields or regulated the pigs in the pig fields. They left it mainly to grass and hay. And to its own devices.

Where the lane joined the Roaring Road it had formed an awkward corner in the field. So awkward, in fact, that it wasn't easy for the humans to get their coughing boxes in and out of it. Perhaps that was why they had let the blackthorn, the dogwood and the elder establish themselves there. Along with any bracken, thorn or bramble that felt at home. The same soil and the same shrubs started up again on the far side of the lane but after a while a banked wall and some new shiny cut them off from more wheatfields, which extended out of Max's territory towards the low horizon where the sun went down.

There were rumours of cows further on from these fields. Chiefly among the hawks and you had to take their high-flown claims with a great deal of scepticism. Still the humans did cut the grass in the meadow and bundle it into hay and load it onto rusty coughing boxes and take it away. So cows there must be. Somewhere.

Right up to the time the humans came to cut the grass down to the roots, this little patch of meadow and scrub maintained a fierce and awkward independence. It teemed with life on the run and life on the make. And, despite it being so close to the Roaring Road, the rabbits found the area wild and free enough to build up extensive warrens.

They dug under the elders, the taste of which they

couldn't stand, as a double bluff to mislead incoming predators. But their bluff was called generations ago. The warrens were a traditional feature of that country now. A resource passed down from hunter to hunter. Stoat families took their young there in early foraging parties, as a matter of course, to let them hone their predatory skills. If he could remember his first kill, it would probably have been a rabbit out of the hayfield warren.

Max left the verge, slipped through the hedgerow and moved up into the field itself. He found the sun had filled it. Buttercups and dandelions pushed up through the glistening grass and over in the corner where the warrens were, the blackthorn was a great white blur of flowers. The soft, warm light hovered over this in pools and whirls, broken up by the colours of the April blooms.

And within a few feet of him in the centre of a sprawling growth of bugle, basking in one unbroken beam of sunlight, lay Sheila. The dark zigzag marking on her back glinted amongst the powder blue flowers.

Sheila was an adult female adder. A vole taker about three times as long as Max with a venomous bite. Adders were retiring by nature. Only the females stood their ground with any intruder and then only when pregnant. Sheila didn't look pregnant; she looked just out of hibernation. But Max couldn't see if she was hungry or not and he held back.

"You're out and about again, are you?" Max didn't expect an answer. Sheila was never much of a conversationalist. She stared at him with torpid eyes, but her disconcerting tongue flickered hesitantly as if she were weighing up whether she was under threat. "It's me. Max."

Sheila eased a coil or two and seemed to relax. The sun was slowly entering her body, driving out the winter cool and the perma-chill of underground. She lay passive beneath this resuscitation until her head finally eased itself up and forward to hover in front of Max's.

The eyes were dead, not questioning but waiting for some spark of reaction to be kindled in them. Max didn't

move. She could be pregnant after all. There was a lot of snake there to pack a few eggs away in. Sheila's tongue stuttered into life again, and Max poised himself for a spring behind her and a bite to the neck. If he could make it, alive.

Sheila bobbed her head and then spoke. "Vole," she said.

"You've had one? Or you want one?" There was a critical distinction. If the adder had just eaten she'd be set for days. And snakes were never ones to waste energy on mindless attacks once they'd eaten. It played havoc with their digestion. If Sheila was full, he could afford to turn his back on her.

"Vole," repeated Sheila and she looked at Max as if he wasn't pulling his weight in the conversation.

"Stoat," corrected Max, tersely.

Sheila stared implacably at him, raising her head a little.

"Stoat, Sheila," he kept it clear and calm. "We've met before."

"Not vole," concluded Sheila and she lay back down for a moment. Then she turned her head back over her coiled body and slithered away under the blue flowers of the bugle patch.

Max counted himself lucky she was still half asleep; although which part of her somnolent mind had thought to ask her prey to identify itself, he wasn't going to go into. He hoped she came to beside a fat bank vole and put them all out of their uncertainty.

He followed the correct survival procedures. He simply refused to believe his eyes and gave her a few more moments to return in a lunging surprise attack. When she didn't, he stood up on his back legs and scanned the meadow. Nothing seemed to be stirring. Anywhere.

They could be slow on the uptake these rabbits. Probably they were only now sensing the warm sunshine at the warren entrances. It would take a few minutes before they started pondering about a breath of fresh air, a little sunlight and some exercise for the babies under Mother's strict supervision.

He made his way towards the tangled scrub in the meadow corner, keeping up a steady pace but careful not to overrun his cover and come into view. The last thing he wanted to do was chase a lot of spooked rabbits round their labyrinth, having to deal with the cornered fury of dominant does and the flaky, last-ditch struggle of full grown bucks. There was an easy way. Taking them one at a time, each out of sight of the other. And that's the way he wanted it done.

As a doe of very low status, Laura wasn't allowed in the main burrow. The dominant does had seized the safest, cosiest nest sites and, not content with that, had forced Laura out to litter in a breeding stop away from the nearest warren entrance.

They'd made it clear she wasn't wanted. They'd half killed her to do it. She'd only stopped her desperate struggle for some safe corner in the warren because she thought she might lose the babies.

Maternity had overcome her survival instincts.

Now she was supposed to draw the teeth away from those pompous kitten-chutes below. She was good enough to be taken by the same bucks; indeed her kittens had the same father as several of the fat fluffy-bottoms below. But while she had been good enough to breed through, now all she was good for was drawing Blood and Guts gang members away from the privileged ones. She and her lovely little ones were stoat fodder.

The bucks had just looked on, of course, as the other does had evicted her. Once they'd mated they lost all interest. Keeping the community in order was left to the females and they took a vindictive pleasure in doing it. Their young came first and hers had to die to protect them.

In her bitterness she hoped the foxes would get in by a back way and tear them all to shreds, all the fat mothers, pampered babies and indifferent fathers. But then within moments she regretted the thought. Her little ones would need a community to thrive in, if they survived.

Donna nudged Danny and Grant out of the way to nuzzle into some warm air seeping in from above their small out burrow. Donna was definitely the brightest and Laura took special pains to ensure she'd suckled enough. Now, even though they were weaned, she felt a mother's responsibility to keep them eating healthily and with eyes in the back of their heads.

She wouldn't always be there, and one day, something murderous would be and they had to be aware enough and fast enough to evade it. That's all a rabbit could do, eat, escape and bring on the future generations.

"Mum," Donna was peering up towards ground level. "It's warm and bright. Can we see?"

"Let's go play out," Grant was up and scrabbling towards the light. Laura pushed brusquely past him to check for incoming teeth and he fell back, too excited by the prospect of tearing around Up Above to sulk at his mother's peremptory treatment.

She sniffed the air, looked around at the main warren doorway and saw that none of the fat mothers were out yet. Mark, a buck she knew, was standing surveying the scene, drinking in the sunshine, and she supposed that was signal enough. Mark was the father of Peggy's latest litter and Peggy was the Leaderene of the doe pack who'd thrown Laura out of the warren. So, in a sense, Mark was the most senior guard the warren could muster.

Danny and Grant bounded out of the burrow and then stood stock-still, overwhelmed by the space and the shape of the great Up Above. They sniffed rapidly and jostled each other for front position in this the world of opportunity.

Laura looked over to Mark but he stared straight through her. The does down below had done their job well. She turned and marshalled her litter. "Stick close to me. Don't run off. Are you listening to me, Grant?"

As ever Grant's boundless energy was driving him off track. He took a series of jerky jumps in the direction of the Roaring Road and then stopped, breathing excitedly through flared nostrils. Then Danny followed up behind.

"Where you going?" asked Danny breathlessly. All that lay ahead was scrubby grass and the hedgerow with its smothering of white blackthorn flowers. And beyond that the mysterious peril of the Roaring Road. Still he assumed his bigger brother had a plan.

Grant turned suddenly and took two hops back in the opposite direction. "Let's go down the centre. See who fancies hanging out up here."

"Not allowed, are we?"

"Oh yeah?" Grant stood up and sniffed the air keenly. The air and the sunlight had given him a confidence boost to match the surge of energy that had accompanied him from Down Below. He felt grown up. "Who says?"

"You know. Mum and Peggy had a big row. And Mum was 'simply impossible'. And Auntie Christine and Mo and Cindy and the rest won't let us down there any more. We're not their sort of rabbits." Danny had collected this information piece-meal from snippets of conversation he'd picked up hiding beside the warren on his last trip up. It had to be true. Grown ups had said it.

"I'm not anybody's sort of rabbit, Danny. I'm my sort of rabbit and they can lump it," Grant declared hotly, before taking an exploratory nibble at what turned out to be a broken twig. He spat it out.

"Come here you two! Right now!" Laura's anxious voice carried over to them. Grant looked sadly and conspiratorially at his smaller brother. "She's messed it up enough for us. And I'm not going to let her stand in my way with her stupid quarrels."

Donna hopped up beside them anxiously scanning the nearest dogwood clump for threats and dangers. "Come on back, Mum's going mad!" she urged, then turned and wrinkled her nose towards the big patch of bramble beside the hedgerow a way back up the field. "There's something nasty here. I know it!"

Max sank down amongst the bramble and calculated the food value in front of him. He'd need to take down two for a proper meal and the chances of that were slim. He might have to wait until someone more substantial hopped into the killing zone for a quiet chew of the grass.

The two young males gave snorts of derision at Donna playing the fearless Warren Guard. She was a bright girl, but she was a girl and that was the end of it. Self-preservation for her meant finding a buck strong enough to breed with and with enough face to set her up comfortably high in the warren community.

Still, Donna's nagging would only be followed by a double helping from their mother and it was too lovely a day to be bossed around. So Grant led Danny back towards their breeding stop, much to their mother's relief. But the sunlight had got hold of him now and he veered off at the last minute and made for the main warren entrance.

Laura was going to cry out, to get them to come back to their proper station in life, but she caught the guard buck's contemptuous smirk and realised she wasn't going to give him the satisfaction.

Mark watched the young rabbits coming towards him and stood tall to give them his most disdainful look. "Where'd you think you're going?"

"See my Aunt Christine," Grant replied sullenly, avoiding the adult's eye. Danny had scampered behind his brother and huddled in. Max watched Donna still scanning her surroundings nearer the hedgerow whilst her mother hopped tentatively towards Danny and Grant and the looming Mark.

"Not down there, you're not." Mark looked dismissively over their heads. "You're not welcome."

"We got relations. And mates. Down there." Danny protested from behind Grant's sulky slumped form, suddenly emboldened by the unfairness of it all.

"You'll have to wait for them to come up. Nobody's going down."

"You're stinky to us and you're stinky to our Mum! You're just a big stinky!" Danny was quivering now and

Grant turned round in amazement at the vehemence of his brother's outburst. He waited for the buck's terrible anger, completely out of his depth but bound to his brother in love and fear.

Laura leapt into the group now, nervous strain pulling her ears back. She was scared the buck might go for her but even more scared he'd attack the boys, so she slipped in low into Mark's fighting space. "Leave it, Mark," she implored.

"They're good boys. Good as gold, Mark."

"They want a good hiding, Laura. You're not dragging them up right." Mark leant over her. "Maybe you want a good hiding yourself."

Laura crouched meekly at his feet. She knew the only way to defuse the situation was to pander to his brittle self importance and get her family back to the relative safety of their own small burrow. "Let me take them out of your way!"

Max moved fast and low away from the bramble patch and into the dogwood between Donna and the commotion at the warren's entrance. He wanted to set himself between the young female and any safe bolthole. With him in the dogwood, she'd never make the warren and from the sound of things she wasn't welcome there anyway. He just needed to head her off from the burrow she'd come out of.

She was little bigger than a baby but she'd do for a start. And once the panic had died down, he'd be back for a bigger one.

"I don't want to go out of his way!" said Grant. "I want to go and see my mates. Down there."

Donna turned back towards the family burrow. Something was making her uneasy in the field and she wanted to think about it in a place of safety. She'd call her Mum back too; together they might work out what was troubling her.

"Grant! Mind your manners!" Laura was wide-eyed in alarm at Grant's behaviour. She glanced up to see how Mark was reacting. "Go home. Before I box your ears."

The buck loosened his shoulders, "Think I'll save you the bother, Laura," he said and Grant shrunk into the ground with Danny, waiting for the pain to start.

Donna was hopping back to the burrow in quick purposeful bounds. She was just opening her mouth to call to her Mum when Max streaked from the dogwood.

Both Mark and Laura picked him up instantly and Mark drummed a frantic warning on the warren's entrance. His defence mechanisms were so deeply ingrained that he let Danny and Grant shoot between his legs and down to safety.

But Laura saw more than a stoat. She saw her daughter, the bright flower of her litter, jumping heedless and defenceless into its path. "Donna!" she screamed. "Watch out!"

Donna pirouetted in a small dust cloud just as Max raced into his launching stance directly in front of her. He skidded to the right, trying to compensate for her sharp turn, and then her back legs buffeted him in the eyes as Donna cut loose for the hedgerow.

Donna didn't know where she was going. After all she hadn't been anywhere yet. But she was going as far away from the slashing teeth of the sleek murderer behind her as possible. And she was going at lung bursting speed. Her sole thought was flight. She had no direction, no plan, just plain flight as death streaked behind her, powerful and focused and closing the gap.

She tried to turn into the field, hoping to make her way back to the main warren and the outside chance of plunging into the labyrinth and the ancient safety of Down Below. But death managed a faster turn and cut her off and she had to pull her body through a muscle tearing counter turn to get clear of it.

She dodged and jinked her way back towards the hedgerow. It seemed to race up to meet her and then, with no idea of what was in front off her, her terror of what was behind propelled her through the slats and the shiny and the tangled leaves with the speed of the possessed.

Donna flew out onto the Roaring Road. Her racing mind had less than a second to register the scale and perspective of this wholly new landscape before she landed, skidded and then leapt towards the far side. With a loud bang she immediately crashed headlong into a coughing box that was hurtling down the road at its own unnatural velocity.

Stunned and in a momentum not of her own, she glanced off the shiny side of the coughing box and was spun down into an agonising impact with the Roaring Road itself. This new collision bounced her up again into the side of the spinning back wheel. From there she was flung in a bone-jarring arc back along the road to bounce herself to a broken halt.

And the pain passed from excruciating to all enveloping and then pounded her into numbness and then there was nothing.

Max heard the impact as he entered the hedgerow at speed. He made the verge in time to see Donna ricocheting down the road and the coughing box swerving off to one side and pulling up with a shriek. He crouched low and backed into the hedge to see what the humans' next move would be. If they moved off again, he'd drag Donna over to the far verge and consume her there. Keeping her death smell as far from the anxious noses back in the warren as possible. No sense in adding to their state of alertness.

Then, at the moment that Donna flopped back into her final small spasm, Ray the crow landed right beside the trembling body and gave it an investigative poke.

Max looked out from the hedgerow in both anger and disbelief. Anger that his prize should be pulled away by a carrion thief. And disbelief because Ray was on his own. The unthinkable had happened and Brian had let Ray out on his own.

Ray gave Donna another exploratory jab with his beak and scuttled around to the other side of her to see if she was wincing at his attentions and needed finishing off. He was evidently satisfied that she was finished already because he settled down to the task of pulling the skin away from her belly.

"Bugger off!" A human female was running up from the coughing box. She looked flushed and worried.

Ray nimbly stepped around the other side of the body and assumed the human would keep going and pass him by. He got on with tearing a way into Donna's abdomen and when he looked up and saw the human towering over him, he gave a disconcerted squawk and sprinted a few feet away. Surely this human wasn't going to steal his broken baby rabbit? They didn't eat things on the Roaring Road. As he looked at her he could feel his confusion being fed with growing irritation.

"Bugger off! You horrible bird," the human female shouted and waved her arms, and stamped her feet hard on the Roaring Road as she marched towards him.

Ray took a few hasty steps backwards and when he'd established that the human female was seriously making for him, he took off and flew into the lower branches of an elder across the road. There he settled and waited calmly for her and her madness to pass.

"Horrible ugly horrible thing!" the human female shouted up at him and then she started to sob and pulled some white fluttery out of somewhere and wiped at her face with it. She didn't seem all that triumphant to have collared his kill for herself, thought Max, but at least she'd seen Ray off for the time being.

She crouched down by Donna and peered closely at her, holding the white fluttery over her mouth. She shook her head.

A little human female got out of the coughing box, followed by a tiny male. The little human female pulled the tiny male onto the verge and held his hand. Then she called out to the adult female examining Donna.

"Mum? Is it going to be alright?"

The female turned quickly, "Rachael! Get back in the car!"

"Good idea. Why don't you all go?" shouted Ray in an evil temper, from the safety of his branch. The adult human flinched at the sound of his voice but made no reply.

"James says he wants to be sick," Rachael explained hopefully.

"Wabbit!" said James delightedly.

The adult female stood up and dodged about from foot to foot in an indecisive manner, looking from the crow to Donna to her own young. Then suddenly she raced back to the coughing box and started to push the little ones back in.

"I'm going to leave it by the side of the road to get better," she said hastily. "We've got to get home and get daddy's dinner."

"S'only lunchtime," objected Rachael. "Daddy's not home for hours."

"Just get James belted in, Rachael." She had closed the door again and was talking loudly through the look-through. "And stop asking questions."

"Not asking questions." Rachael's muffled voice came from the car.

"Wabbit?" James sounded petulant. "Wabbit."

The human female walked up to where Donna lay and then turned to look back at the coughing box. There was no sight or sound of her young and so with an awkward movement she gave Donna a sudden toe-poke towards the roadside.

Donna didn't move. She seemed stuck to the road although, as Max could see, there was hardly any blood and no guts involved in the situation yet. The human female shuddered and tried again and Donna turned over into an untidy bundle.

The human female stuck her foot out far in front of her and tried to push Donna towards the verge but Donna kept turning aside from her foot and seemed to be revolving in gritty circles. The human female persisted, with intermittent glances back towards the coughing box to make sure her own young were safely tucked away.

Then with a small gasp of exasperation she gave a big shrug and a shake of her head and rushed back to the coughing box. She was inside in seconds and the coughing box moved away equally quickly.

There was a lot of talking going on inside but Max lost it in the rush. He raced down the verge to the spot opposite Donna's final, dusty, resting-place, only to find Ray had already arrived.

Ray was continuing his excavating work in Donna's insides. He looked up briefly as he registered Max in the ragwort on the verge opposite.

"See that, Max?" he barked in outraged disbelief. "Wossa point of kicking a dead rabbit? Only spreads it out."

"That's my kill, Ray."

"Just makin' life difficult. Typical, innit?" Ray tore at Donna's intestines and then registered Max's claim. "Oh no, Max. Come off a coughing box this one."

"I drove it here. I had it. That human just took it off me."

"Nicked it and kicked it, eh?" Ray gave a cheery snort and then fixed Max with a lethal and proprietorial stare. "Plenty more back there, mate."

Max wasn't about to scrabble in the Roaring Road for a replaceable dinner. Ray was unbalanced at the best of times. It was only his brother Brian who kept him operating within close proximity to sanity. Which reminded him about Brian, and Ray's startling solo appearance here.

"Where's Brian?"

"Eh?"

"Brian? He let you out on your own?"

Ray laughed outright at this absurd suggestion. "Don't talk mental."

"Not normally on your own, though, are you?"

"Catch him down here. She's got him all tied up at home."

"Who has?"

"Her in the nest." Ray shook his head at his brother's stupidity. "He lets her walk all over him. Got him hanging round the nest. Feeding her bugs and suchlike."

So the ice-cold killer of the treetops and roadside was bustling round behind his egglayer like a blackbird or a hedge sparrow. The power of the egg.

"Well," said Max, "once they get eggs...."

"Females. Can't live with 'em; can't live without 'em." pronounced Ray in a worldly fashion. A length of Donna's gut trailed out of one side of his beak and he tried to stand on it and pull it clear.

This surprised Max. He hadn't thought Ray would be the mating type. Even if a female crow was demented enough to let him within five trees of her. "You got one, then, Ray?"

"I don't flappin' want one," Ray shouted forcibly. It was clearly a big issue with him. He looked at Max as if the stoat had lost his reason. "What'd I need a female for?" And then he pointed out with laboured clarity, "Got this rabbit, ain't I?"

"Right," agreed Max. Nobody had lost their mind and mated with Ray after all. There was some balance in nature.

He backed into the hedge, leaving Ray with his spoils of the afternoon; a bleeding, gravel scraped substitute for a mate and young, while his bigger brother was nest bound and hen-pecked. Not that anybody would ever say that to Brian, but it would be good to remember, the next time the murderous crow strutted by.

Ray forgot Max the moment he disappeared back into the hedgerow by the hayfield.

And Laura didn't see him as she hopped nervously along the hedgerow on the field side, peering anxiously into the leaves. Her heart was aching with fear for her daughter but a wild recklessness, the need for a mother to know, drove her on in the hope she would discover Donna alive.

"Donna?" she whispered into the hedge around the

place she thought she had seen her baby disappear. "Donna, it's Mum. You can come out now."

She peered at the hedge in sad desperation, skimming over Max's position without a momentary pause. Her sense of smell and her sense of danger wafted away by the April breeze and a mother's refusal to countenance the death of a favourite child.

Max watched the quivering nose, the yearning eyes, as Laura softly trod towards him.

He adjusted his weight onto his back feet and readied himself for the kill.

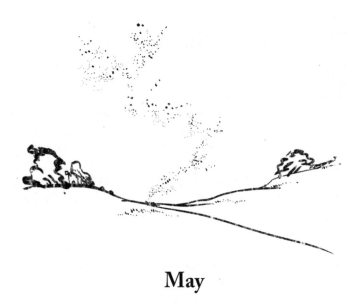

# May

## Love is in the Air

The sun was high; the day was late spring warm. A light breeze batted the butterflies off their flight paths amongst the tall grasses and adder tongue ferns of the meadowland.

Max kept to every available shadow as he coursed the old wall the humans had placed between the hayfield and the stream that run all the way down from the Oak Wood.

The stream went on for a very long run, right over to the big duckpond near where the humans had their burrows and their little flower-fields. But the old wall only lasted the length of the hayfield down to the lane, while the stream went under the Lane itself and then came up on the other side, smelling no different but not quite as clear, as it moved on to its journey's end.

As he moved up the slight gradient through the coarse grass at the wall's base, listening to the light burble of the stream on the other side, Max wondered why the humans had put the wall there at all.

They didn't live in it, like their burrows. And it was fallen down in places, where they'd jabbed in big sticks and tangles of sharp shiny and the nettles and bracken had packed in the spaces in between.

Of course there was always a way through. Except for the one break where Don the badger ran, and nobody in his or her right mind went near there, the smell of murder being all round the place.

Still if the humans didn't live in it, voles and mice did. And the odd bird and maybe even a rabbit or two. And any of that meant lunch. Providing there were no unpleasant surprises.

He drew up short as the wall broke down into the next tangle of sharp shiny and nettles. The light, airy scent of the bankside wafted through the bracken towards him.

It brought with it a distant clamour of tiny voices, punctuated with little happy shouts and exclamations.

Max checked the sky and as much as he could smell of the hayfield, then stepped tentatively out from the wall's end onto the trampled meadow grass in front of the break. (There'd been a lot of traffic through here, clearly. And some of it might still be lying in wait.)

The little, clamouring voices were close enough for him to decide that the owners were probably too small to be mortal threats. But they were too far away to work out what they were, how many of them there were, and if they were edible.

He was about to slip through the bracken to investigate when a flinty and unpleasantly close voice erupted from under the grass he was standing on.

"Get off out of it, you!" it shrieked.

Max sprang back, fangs bared, when a similar voice flew up from right beside the first.

"Oh yeah? You're history, pal!"

The first voice grated across the new one immediately, "I'll sort you out right now, mate!"

Max crept silently back onto the rocky outcrop at the

jagged end of the wall. He peered intently into the flattened grass, searching desperately to detect even the most fleeting movement. Only the shrill, enraged voices leapt up at him.

"You male or female?"

"Keep your nose out of my business, while you still got it."

"Don't matter anyway. You're in the wrong place at the wrong time. You're dead meat."

"Wrong place? Me! Wrong place!" Whatever it was became beside itself with fury. "I'll rip your shrewin' lungs out!"

Shrews, thought Max. Vicious, spiteful, incensed things. Forever shrieking and spitting but tiny for all that. If they got their teeth into each other, he could bite through them in a moment. Provided he could find them. He lowered his head to sniff the grass cover cautiously.

"Wassat smell?" one screamed immediately. "Stoat, is it? Shrewin' stoat sticking his big nose in?"

"How would you know?" spat the other. "You couldn't smell your own rear end."

"Stoat or not, I'll have him! Once I done you."

Max drew his head back slightly and then stabbed down through the grass, going for a killer bite at the voice. As he broke the surface he sensed a tiny, scrabbling retreat, but pulled back immediately. Head down in flattened grass was a vulnerable place to be – and a shrew in his eyes or a sparrowhawk on his back was the last thing he wanted. All Max wanted was lunch.

"Oi! Stoat! Shrew off or I'll kill you!" came a distant but still enraged threat.

"Not with no lungs you won't," replied the other and off they went again.

"Don't make me laugh!"

"Right, you're dead!"

Max left them to it. He wasn't that hungry, yet. He turned and slipped through the tangle of sharp shiny and bracken, towards the crowd of clamouring voices and the lapping of the stream.

Once through the wall break, he was engulfed in the riot of water cresses, willowherb and sedge that tumbled over the bankside into the stream itself.

Protected from the sun by all this matted vegetation, the bankside soil was still moist and the light was dim and he could barely hear the clamouring crowd. But even in the dense, cool, green mass, he found the bodies soon enough.

There were three of them. Two in the mud and one suspended in some unyielding cow parsley. All three were babies, with fragile, spindly bones and frail, distended gut sacs already perforated and reduced by the local mud scuttlers.

Their oversized beaks craned in different directions from weak shoulders. The two who lay close to the earth gazed along the mud path, appraising long passed dangers with filmy and sightless eyes. The third hung head down from its parsley perch and stared emptily back over its shoulder towards the sky.

Three wagtail babies. No use at all. There wasn't a real bite in a live one, much less in these leaf thin skin bundles. He'd have been better off with the shrews.

Max nosed one aside impatiently and moved on through the next sedge clump to find himself, with a start, breaking cover into a sun dappled patch of bankside mud.

He knew at once he'd been spotted.

This had nothing to do with the clamouring voices.

It had everything to do with a small dark hole in the bank opposite. There was something bright and small set back in it. Which glinted and then disappeared.

Max shrunk down and watched for the glint to reappear. Until it turned into an eye. And a small face framed itself around it as the animal moved slowly towards the daylight.

It was a grave round face, with whiskers. Small, neat ears and thick silky hair. It was a water rat.

The two animals stood and regarded each other cautiously.

"Hullo, Max," said the water rat.

"Hallo Dave," said Max. They were quite tasty, water rats, more to them than your bank vole.

"Bit off your stretch, aren't you, Max?" said the rat evenly. He knew how wide his stream was. "What you doing messing around here?"

"I never mess around, Dave," replied Max, deciding the stream was too wide to chance it.

"Bit of local business, then."

"Something like that."

The clamouring voices seemed suddenly to have come much closer to them. A deluge of sound, of yells and laughs. Max turned to look down stream. Now he was out of the sedge he had an ominously clear line of vision.

Just downstream was a cloud of insects, like wisp upon wisp of smoke turning in and over upon itself. The bottom-most part of it hovered just above the surface of the stream itself. And despite all the hundreds involved, no collisions, no noticeable fights; just an ever changing formation of noisy, writhing wing-borne bugs.

"What's all that then, Dave?" he'd instinctively crouched back ready to bite his way back to the safe darkness of the dead wagtails.

"That lot?" Dave seemed only mildly interested, but then he only ate plants. "That's just the Mayflies."

"Make a lot of noise for insects," said Max, wincing at the jabbering throng. "How d'you manage to sleep round here?"

"Never see them normally," said Dave, sniffing the air suspiciously. This was a long and vulnerable conversation for a water vole. "Nothing all year. Then whoosh. Up they come from the water. Letting rip."

He brought his fore-paws to the rim of the hole in the bank. Max reminded himself he'd never heard of a water rat taking on one of the Blood and Guts department. But still.

"This is their big day," said Dave.

Then, plop! Dave was gone. Out from his hole and straight down into the water. Max waited for him to break the surface. Perhaps to rear up just before him, snarling and deranged.

But the stream ran sweetly on.

Max slipped cautiously into the next riot of bankside plants, moving closer to the mayfly cloud.

All those insects must attract insect-eaters. As it was too bright for badgers, and provided he watched out for air attack, Max felt sure he could make a reasonable lunch out of an insect-eater.

He advanced warily. But his hunger was beginning to gnaw at him.

A few meters down the bank from Dave's hole, almost under the insect cloud itself, Shane struggled out of his old dun suit. Then leaving that last shabby part of the old him lying in the obscurity of some damp leaf mould, he made straight up for the noise and the bright lights.

This was it. No more kid stuff in the bottom of some gloomy pond. No more adolescent mooching about, just getting by. This was it, alright. Party Time. And he was ready to go for it.

"Here I come," he yelled as the oxygen rushed into his lungs. "Here I come. Sex on wings."

They were all around him. The Party Generation. In their hundreds. It was a writhing festival of light and love. Of pure desire. What else was there? Their voices filled the sky. One of them was his lover. He had to find her.

Their wings were dazzling. Their voices were music in the air. He soared through them. Amongst them.

"We're going to do it! We're really going to do it."

"I love you. I want you!"

"I'm over here."

"Not you. You!"

The Party Generation danced about him. Shane hovered on delirious wings and then darted upward to new friends and new possibilities. He was a mayfly. He was a Party Insect. Where was the Mayfly of His Dreams?

"Over here!"

"I'm yours."

"Mine?"

"No, his."

He bustled up through the throng. Quite a few had sorted themselves out already. They cascaded past in windborne ecstasy. Doing what he was dying for. It only increased his anticipation. He veered from one group to the next. Swirl after swirl. She was here somewhere.

"I can't believe this is happening!"

"Oh please! Please!"

"Excuse me!"

"I love everybody!"

"I never knew it would be like this!"

"Over here!"

Shane crested the top of the party. The highest he'd ever flown. Circling breathlessly, he looked down through the cloud of pleasure, seeking a glimpse of her, a clue, anything. He'd have to go back to the bottom and start again. No problem. He knew she was here, waiting to set him alight. He plunged back into the party circuit.

"Oh. I just can't stand it."

"Over here."

"Oh yes, please!"

"No. Come back."

And then he saw her against the leaf green shadow of (what was it?) a tree. What did he care about trees? He flung himself towards her. She just had to be his.

Then, maddeningly, the Universe shifted. The Party Generation juddered sideways and for a precious second he lost his bearings. He hovered frantically, trying to realign himself and peering through the shimmering wings, the thrashing bodies.

Had he found her just to have her torn away, back into the carnival?

Two grown wagtails settled side by side on a thin branch pointing promisingly over the stream towards Shane and his crowded destiny.

"Just look at them all, Adrian!" The female shook her head emphatically. "How many do you think there are?"

"Loads," replied Adrian, rocking in small eager steps beside her.

"Loads and loads?"

"Enough for our boy, anyway, Judy."

Judy took off, "Adrian, I'm going over here," and darted to the other side of the stream to land on top of the crumbling wall.

"Good thinking, Judy."

"I'm here, OK?"

"OK." Adrian pulled prissily at a wing feather, and then looked at the mayflies. "Lots of them, aren't there?"

"Oh yes," Judy gave a little flutter. "Looks just as many from over here. But, in fact," she took off and darted crosstream again, "I'm coming back to your side," and she landed, "but not the same branch. Here I am."

Adrian took off sharply, "Well, I'm going right where you were." He started but veered off in mid-course. "No I'm not. I'm going to catch one."

And into the Party Generation he swooped.

There she was! There! At last, Shane had his beloved in sight. Stretching himself to the limit, he flew in between a particularly complex shimmer of Partygoers to hover just in front of her. His heart was bursting with love.

"I'm here," he said bashfully.

She turned, and danced in a gentle pattern before him. All the while, she looked steadily at Shane and a stillness descended upon him.

"You're beautiful," she spoke it as a simple truth. "You're absolutely beautif…."

She disappeared from his sight as Adrian took her in mid-flight, his strong beak crushing her body, tearing away her forelegs and leaving the others jerking feebly as they stuck out on either side.

Shane was pushed back by the backdraft of the mottled streak of power that had wiped his beloved from the face of the earth. He was suddenly mobbed by Partygoers and drawn further in to the dance.

"I love you!"

"Did you see that?"

"Do you want me?"

"There was a something… it took my…."

"Come on. Come to me!"

Shane danced, but kept trying to look back. He felt this peculiar incompleteness. Some strange sense of loss. But this was a party. He shrugged away the feeling. He had things to do, right now. Party things.

There was a mayfly here just meant for him, and all he had to do was find her. He took off for the pinnacle of the pleasure cloud again. Sex on wings.

Adrian settled back alongside Judy on her branch. She looked admiringly at the remnants of Shane's Beloved sticking out either side of Adrian's beak.

"That looks like a nice one, Adrian," she said, dipping her head to have a good peer at it.

"It ith, oodee." Adrian's firm grip on the bulk of Shane's Beloved was rather muffling him. "'Ut I eenk I'll 'et a 'ew 'ore. 'E's a 'ig eater our 'oy."

He gave his head a sudden whiplash shake. One of Shane's Beloved's legs detached itself and fell away towards the stream.

"Don't waste it," Judy scolded, watching the leg tumble on the breeze.

"'enty 'ore!" protested Adrian, wounded, and off he suddenly fired himself to prove it.

"He's a big eater, alright," said Judy with a mother's pride. She knew from the moment he'd hatched that her son was rather special. "He's going to need a lot of those."

Adrian pitched a slight variant in his flight path through the cloud, hitting it in the middle and climbing suddenly through it to exit at the top. This allowed him to open his beak at the last possible moment and slam another reveller in on top of Shane's Beloved, using the wind-rush to keep both in place.

Closing his beak proved tougher than expected, and he bit down against a surprising resistance. Still he kept his trap shut, just like his dad had taught him, and landed next to Judy again, with just a bit of a flutter on landing.

Judy was staring at him wide eyed in astonishment. Adrian looked at her curiously. He felt pleased at the attention, but rather awkward with whatever was going on in his mouth.

"You are clever!" exclaimed Judy. "You got two that time."

"I 'ow," he lied. Then before all three dropped out and made a fool of him, he said "'M'off 'ome."

And he took off.

"I'll get some more, then," Judy shouted after him but Adrian was gone. She watched him keep close to the water as he followed the bankside, then jink left up over a sedge clump for his final, fluttering approach along the top of the wall, to the nest where her darling was waiting.

Max saw him too. The wagtail had practically taken his head off as he'd clipped the bankside sedge. Too busy with the mayflies stuffed down its craw, thought Max.

And he remembered the three, scattered, baby corpses back along the bank towards the sharp shiny break in the wall. The place was stiff with wagtails. Admittedly he'd seen more dead than alive. But those dead fledglings meant there had to have been a nest. Perhaps even nests. And if wagtail adults were still plundering the mayfly cloud, then those nests were still there. And they had to be unattended.

And unattended nests meant lunch.

Max turned and worked his way back through the dark, tangled greenery till he found the base of the wall. Then he followed it back in the direction of the sharp shiny break until he found a small, lichen covered fissure. There, looking around to see if anything bigger and nastier than a wagtail was in the air, he started to climb.

From the moment he locked onto the wall's top for his approach, Adrian saw it. The Mouth. He couldn't see the nest as such, just a massive mouth like a great orange beacon which drew him along, ever faster.

The Mouth seemed to sense his approach, too. He was

still feet away when it started up.

"Dad! Dad! Feed me, Dad! Hurry up, Dad! I'm starving! Dad!"

Adrian landed and tried to gain some purchase on the nest. His feet scrabbled for any small space not filled up by his huge son. He popped the first mayfly into the Mouth, in a panicky attempt to give himself some time to arrange his footing. Time was not forthcoming.

The first mayfly didn't touch the sides. "What you got, Dad? Where is it, Dad?" the Mouth grew bigger and bigger.

He shovelled in the next two. The Mouth didn't even seem to swallow them. They simply disappeared.

"Dad! Dad! I'm famished! Haven't you got anything to eat at all, Dad?" It seemed to grow bigger. Adrian pulled his head away, in case he followed the mayflies into his son's ravening hunger.

"Mum's coming. She's got you something," he promised earnestly. "And I'm going to get some more, too."

The Mouth vibrated angrily at him, "But I'm hungry now, Dad! I'm dying of hunger, Dad! Feed me, Dad!" Adrian took off like lightning. He had to fill the Mouth, even if his wings broke up and his lungs burst.

"Hang on, Son," he cried in paternal desperation as he tore into a high speed turn back to the mayfly cloud, "I'll be right back with more!"

"Dad! Feed me, Dad! Dad!" Then, once it sensed its father had gone, the Mouth closed and it settled back to give itself a little preen and a little time to let the mayflies digest.

Adrian and Judy crossed in mid-air, and he saw she had only one mayfly in her beak.

"That's never enough," he shouted over his shoulder as he accelerated towards the mayfly cloud. "We need more, much more."

"Mum! Mum!" The Mouth picked her up immediately as she braked to land. "Feed me, Mum! I'm starving! Dad gave me hardly anything!"

As Judy landed nimbly on her nest, the Mouth flung itself at her. He was such a big boy. And a lovely black colour all over. Not black and white like an ordinary wagtail. She popped the mayfly into the orange gape that threatened to engulf her. The Mouth absorbed it.

"Come on, Mum! Feed me, Mum! You must give me more! More Mum! More!" The Mouth was almost tipping her over the side of the nest in its frenzy of demands.

"You chew your food, properly, Simon," she scolded as she tried to regain her balance, "or you'll get indigestion."

The Mouth swelled and rose above her. Her son was at least twice her size. She'd never seen such a healthy wagtail. He screamed at her. "I can't help it if I'm starving, Mum! It's your fault! Dad takes ages and you shout at me! And I'm dying of hunger!"

Her heart welled over, "Are you, Simon? Are you? Don't worry, Daddy's coming. He's here now."

Adrian scrabbled to land alongside her, three more dead mayflies crammed uncomfortably in his beak. He was still trying to steady himself when the Mouth ripped them from him with such force that Adrian almost fell from the nest. Judy half-fluttered into the air herself and, wings beating clumsily at each other, they managed to take off for the mayfly cloud together.

"Feed me, Dad. Feed me," the Mouth bawled after them.

"I'm dying, Mum! I'm dying!" and then it settled down to wait again.

"I'm coming, Son!" shouted Adrian and he pushed his tormented wing muscles to the limit, to crash dive into the mayfly revellers and pillage them for his boy.

"Oh, I hope he's going to be alright!" cried Judy as she followed him into the heart of the Party Generation. "He's a growing boy, after all."

The Mouth lay contentedly in the warm sunshine. He liked these times to himself, crammed into the cosiness of the nest, dreaming of his future. He was going to have quite a future, he knew. He was cut out for something special. He wasn't going to end up like his shabby little parents, toting bugs about all day. Oh no, he was going places.

His feeding sense picked up an arrival at the nest, and at once he was up and gaping, "Dad! I'm starving! Mum!"

But for once, nobody landed to feed him. Yet there was somebody there. His feeding sense was never wrong.

"Mum? Dad?" he swung his head around, in case they were coming in from a different direction. He didn't like to be messed about like this, but food was food. He felt something on the nest rim behind him and turned immediately and angrily. "Dad! Why've you been so long!"

"My, my," said Max, "aren't you a big boy?"

Max sniffed appreciatively at the cuckoo. This was a stroke of luck. A real bonus. A wagtail brood would simply have tidied him over. But a big bouncing baby cuckoo like this was going to make quite a snack.

Now he knew how the wagtail fledglings had ended up on the bankside. Why hadn't he thought of that before? Still, he was here now. And he was going make the most of it.

The Mouth knew something wasn't quite right here. This new thing was not a wagtail as he knew it. Still, it had arrived at the nest in mid-daylight and his Mum and Dad had not made any fuss, so whatever it was clearly intended to feed him. He puffed himself up into full demand and gaped at the newcomer.

"I'm starving!" he wheedled.

"Me too," replied Max companionably, and bit his head off.

Max chewed on the head indulgently for a minute, before dragging the rest of the carcass along the crest of the wall and down into the fissure he'd climbed up.

He wasn't worried about the return of the wagtails (The more the merrier in fact.) but he knew a sparrowhawk could pluck him off the wall as easily as he'd snatched up the cuckoo chick, whose blood was pumping so delightfully into his nostrils. There was no sense in running risks on top of the wall when he could gorge in peace inside it. Max tucked the two of them into a cosy stone crevice, and bit deep into his lunch.

Like all water rats, Dave was very partial to dropwort. He was whistling lightly through his teeth as he hauled a straggling length out of the bright water and away from the bankside to a favourite patch of willowherb.

There, having checked every close horizon, he settled down for a good old chew. Seeing Max had shaken him. Like any self-respecting water rat, Dave had his escape routes above and below water level, and a run of tunnels that would confuse and demoralise the most persistent of stoats. But still, his face-to-face run in with the flesh ripper had soured his day.

Animals like Max brought the smell of death with them. And even if they'd just eaten and there was no chance of them having a go at you, you just knew that they'd like to. And that felt very unsettling. He chewed every morsel of comfort out of his dropwort, running along the length of the plant frond, paw over paw. This was one of a water rat's few pleasures in life, even if it had to be taken hurriedly and with eyes in your tail.

Still, on a lovely spring day like today, he wasn't going to let a flesh-ripper like Max force him underground into the dark. Not on his own stretch of stream. And with a defiant little snort, Dave chewed with renewed vigour on the next length of dropwort that came to paw.

Across the stream, Max stuck his head out of the fissure in the wall to check for hawks and other problems. He thought he'd see if there were any other wagtail nests along the crest. (Well, he wasn't that hungry but while he was up there, it would be a shame to waste the opportunity.)

That said, he didn't want any unpleasant interruptions. Particularly ones with slashing talons and throat gouging beaks. So he squinted carefully through the cuckoo's blood at the May day all around him.

In his first visual sweep of the far bankside, Max immediately picked up Dave chewing away in his favourite willowherb patch.

"Dave!" he shouted, clearing some feathers and blood from his throat. "Dave!"

Dave twitched, threw aside his dropwort and cast around himself frantically, trying to identify the threat. He dashed to the bankside, preparing to dive.

"Dave!" shouted Max. "I'm on the wall!"

Dave's squinting eyes raked the crumbling surface, left to right, right to left, working upwards desperately. Couldn't be a sparrow hawk, he wouldn't have got a warning. He wouldn't be around to terrify himself like this. Then he spotted Max's bullet head framed by the May sunshine at the wall's crest.

He blanched at the stoat's tight, blood-smeared smile, "Is that you, Max?" The animal appeared to be wearing something's insides. "What do you want?"

Max looked down, serenely. "I can see your house from here."

And then he was gone.

# June

## A Light Roadside Lunch

It was a time of flowers. Flowers and caterpillars. Blooms and insects. The mid-summer sun beat down on the honeysuckle blooming around the human burrows up by the green patch and the poppies in the hayfields and the pink foxgloves in the Oak Wood. And Frank the blackbird was feeling overwhelmed.

He perched in the top of the hawthorn bush and said as much.

"Where do they all flapping come from? That's what I want to know."

The humans had invaded. They came in long streams of coughing boxes down through the Oak Wood along the Roaring Road and all over the countryside. They tramped through the fields in groups, sending the rodent population trembling into deep cover. They sat around the duckpond and threw enormous amounts of food to the gasping inhabitants, most of which sank to the bottom to rot. They walked the lanes, unsettling the finches and the linnets with nestlings to feed.

In short, they got in the way. While it had to be admitted that the food they dropped and the scuffed up tracks they left in the fields provided a healthy summer diet for all sorts, there was always another human coming along to disturb the creatures feeding off the residue of the last.

They arrived without warning, they interfered and then they moved on in a deluge of unwanted shiny and crinkly and broken look-through.

Right now a steady trickle of coughing boxes oozed along the Roaring Road throwing up a dense smell of hot oily. Already that morning one had stopped and made steam and noise and the humans had got out and shouted at each other. And another bigger coughing box had come and pulled it away to the human burrow far down the Roaring Road, which smelt of oily too and had lights on all night.

A lot of coughing boxes clustered like insects around this burrow. And then rushed away like angry hornets. Perhaps the one with the noise and steam would do the same down there.

Frank sighed heavily, "The tits are all over the caterpillars in the woods, but do they go and disturb them?"

Max looked up from his shady place in a tangle of burdock and goose grass near the rotting food box. "There's sharp shiny on the way into the Oak Wood. Most humans don't like sharp shiny."

"Why'd they string it everywhere then?" Frank gave his right wingpit a tentative preen, then stopped and considered, "They don't make any real sense, do they?"

Max didn't even bother to answer. It was too hot to speculate on the continual mysteries of human life. If mysteries they were. Humans came along. They made things difficult. They left.

Not much of a mystery to that.

If you wanted to survive you kept out of their way until

such times as your country stopped providing you with food. Then, and only then, you had to creep in close to some humans and steal some of theirs.

Luckily they threw so much away you didn't usually have to sneak in too close. You could generally give their burrows a wide berth for example. Unless it was night, of course.

Most humans were useless at night. They clearly never got hungry enough to go for the kill after dark.

Frank had got tired of his one-way conversation. "I could do this all day, Max," he said with heavy irony. "But I really must get something done."

"Back up the Pig Killers', again?" Max watched the blackbird jump to the farm side of the hawthorn.

"It's smelly, but they're putting out all kinds of goodies for the fatties," he explained. "Too good for pigs at any rate."

He flew off and had cleared the apple trees on his way to the pig fields when the little red coughing box appeared on the Roaring Road, coughing its way out of the Oak Wood.

It was crammed full with humans. The roof was piled high with wobbling smaller boxes, all tied together with bright green stretchy. The red and the green glinted and dazzled in the bright sunlight.

Max watched it pull wearily into the lay-by and come to a jerky halt only a few feet away from the rotting food box and a reasonably safe distance from his ambush point.

The moment the coughing box stopped, the doors sprung open and out burst a human family, standing, stretching, scratching and blinking in the bright early afternoon sunshine. It was a hot day for the time of the year and it showed in their shiny faces, and their sweet and yeasty smell.

Max watched intently, hardly breathing, as the two biggest humans walked round to the back of the coughing box and opened the little door there. They began to unload boxes and rest-ons and covers and other human objects.

"I'll manage the table," said the big male to the smaller female,   "You drag out those chairs."

An even smaller female then got out of the coughing box, moved dodderingly over to one of the chairs which the younger female had provided. She sat down on it heavily.

Suddenly two noisy, tiny human young scrambled out and disappeared behind a large and scrappy hawthorn bush. They were out of sight, but Max could hear them rummaging around in there and he knew they weren't coming out for a while. He checked around his line of vision, though, just in case he'd been spotted himself, before raising his head a little higher.

The two biggest humans had settled now, sitting at their table, helping the smaller doddery one fiddle with their boxes. They passed round flat things and shiny things, unwrapped glittering parcels and opened bright orange boxes. Max sniffed the air. That confirmed it.

"Right, that's it," he said, "they're eating."

From the shade of his nearby log, sunk in the bracken that clogged the drainage ditch behind the rotting food box, Ted the toad raised a tentative question.

"Hmm-ah," he cleared his throat, "when did you last eat, Max?"

Max crouched back down, and turned towards Ted's log. "We've been through all that, Ted. It was a mistake and… to be fair, you got away."

Ted stretched out his long toad's tongue and pondered.

"You don't have to worry about me," Max continued more sharply now, tired of the apology. "You taste disgusting."

"Tell all your friends," said Ted, rolling his tongue back into the shade. He watched Max raise himself back up on his hind legs to peer at the eaters again. "They got anything worth knowing about? Any worms?"

Max gave the picnic a full going over with his nose, "Old meat…. Hot leaves in water…. That sweet sticky rotten fruit they're so fond of…. Nothing for you."

"Sweet and sticky, eh? It'll get busy, then," Ted sighed heavily. "We'll have that Waldo over again. Stirring things up."

"Here we go," said Max, eyes narrowing, "the ants are out already."

Two flying advance columns, black and bustling, clambered out of their kerbside bunkers, reformed and struck out purposefully for the eating humans at their table.

"Might be a snack in it for me then," said Ted hopefully. "Few wayward ants wouldn't go amiss."

"If they're making the usual mess, they'll leave enough to bring the mice out," said Max. He spoke almost to himself, hunger rising. "Do with a mouse. Or a couple of voles."

"Try and remember that, will you?" said Ted, pointedly. "Voles, yes. Toads, no."

"Look, I'm a stoat," hissed Max. "When I get hungry, I get nasty. Nothing I can do about it."

"Come on, come one, move it!" A cruel and raucous voice cut in from overhead. "We don't want those little mud-scuttlers all over it before we get there."

Waldo the wasp and his ill-tempered squadron hedge-hopped above Max's ears, speeding like dirty bullets towards the picnic and leaving a relentless buzzing in their wake.

They circled the family, instinctively out of range of the flapping hands, trying to get a proper aerial picture of the target.

"Right, split up," Waldo snapped. "I'm going in for a closer look at that orange pot."

Waldo hovered inches above the table top, and then threw himself into a backward roll as a paper napkin swept down out of the sun at him. He chuckled evilly and put himself into a breathtaking climb, firing instructions to the rest of his flight.

"Jason, Martin, you keep the big one busy, it's slow but it don't know it. Darren, Stu, Keef, the rest of you come in under that smaller one. It's all over the place. Really shaky. We'll have it off that butter in no time."

He flew a triumphant circle above the big one's head, giving his final directions, "Remember your training. Standard picnic procedure. Everybody draws attention from everybody else," he spat, "Let's do it. Let's eat." and launched himself into a power dive.

As the wasps attacked, Stan the sparrow, his wife Jean and her brother Morris landed scrappily in the soft dust near the rotting food box and hopped nervously around, cheeping to each other as they scanned the bushes for cats and other unwelcome guests. Stan picked up Max's fixed gaze at once.

"Wotcha, Max," he said brightly. Loud enough to make sure that Jean and Morris immediately hopped a few feet further away from Max and a few feet nearer to the picnic.

"Hello Stan," Max resisted licking his lips. "How's the family?"

"Same as ever." Stan settled happily into a small dust-bowl a careful distance away from Max's clump of burdock. "Noisy, hungry and hopping all over the place." He flapped his wings busily, throwing up clouds of dirt and dust over his head.

"Oooh. That's better."

Max edged silently to the outermost limit of his burdock patch. Still safe from prying eyes, he measured the distance between Stan's dust bath and himself. With the right sprinting start, this was going to be a doddle.

"These fleas never let up, do they?" Stan cheeped cheerfully from the centre of his little cloud.

"Murder, isn't it?" Max agreed sociably, easing his weight onto his forepaws as his back legs flexed for take-off.

"Nice talking to you, Max," said Stan, hopping smartly out of his cloud, and landing a few inches just too far away. "Only, you know my lot. Can't leave them alone for a moment."

Max relaxed his muscles, no point now.

"Get into no end of bother otherwise," said Stan chirpily, hopping towards the picnic. "Take care, Max."

"And you, Stan," said Max. That was that. He'd have to hang around for the mice.

And if the mice didn't show up, he'd have to wait till nightfall and try his luck dragging down some big buck rabbit or a hare in the fields behind. It'd take a lot more effort, in the dark, with most of the rabbits fully grown, but anything would be an improvement on taking another bite out of Ted.

"Auntie! For crying out loud, cover the jam pot!" Violence suddenly erupted at the picnic table. The big male was lashing around him with the top of an orange shiny box, whilst the female made screeching noises at him. "Careful Tony, you'll brain someone!"

"These wasps, they're everywhere," complained the big male still thrashing the air with his plastic lid. "I knew we shouldn't have stopped. Gotcha!"

Jason had lost his concentration, being so intoxicatingly close to a spoonful of jam and the big one had caught him a hefty sideswipe. He careened out of the sky to the dust below.

"Leave him, Keef!" snapped Waldo. "Don't lose formation, the big one'll just pick us off."

Jason crashed, stunned, into the gravel. He buzzed feebly in the dirt, trying to focus and gather his wits about him for a desperate take-off attempt. Max could hear Ted inch a little way out from under his log.

"Sounds promising," the toad called out to Max. "Casualties, are there?"

"Euuh! Dirty horrid things!" the doddery picnicker called Auntie shook with disgust, as she stamped her foot down hard on the woozy wasp and squidged it hard from side to side.

"There's one down," reported Max, watching closely, "but he's in a dreadful state. Spread out all over the place."

"Crying shame. Those ants'll have him broken down and shipped out in no time."

"Don't think the ants'll be able to find him. Treatment he's getting," said Max, as Auntie squidged on and on and on. "That human's going to an awful lot of trouble killing something it's not even going to eat."

"Gives me the creeps the way they do that," agreed Ted. "It's a total waste of a perfectly good wasp."

"There's plenty more," said Max, watching Waldo renewing the attack. "You might get lucky."

"The way I see it," continued Ted, "if you're not going to eat a wasp, leave it alone for someone who will."

Suddenly shrill squeals of fear and disgust poured out of the hawthorn bush. They came from one of the two tiny ones as she crashed blindly out through the leaves and branches, her frock all muddy and tangled.

"Daddy! Daddy! Stephen's found a dead bird," she howled.

"Come out of there, Stephen." The big male roared immediately.

The tiny one sat on a chair and immediately stuffed something to eat in her mouth. Slightly muffled, she continued her dreadful story. "It's a big dead bird. With all its insides out. All mashed up. And he picked it up."

"How did I miss that?" thought Max and then he wondered how many others around the lay-by were thinking the same thing. He felt a deeply aggrieved anger rising with his hunger. It caused him to speak out loud, "I went through that bush this morning. Not a sniff of a dead bird. Now some little human's got his teeth into it."

"My wasp, your bird," Ted agreed morosely.

"Stephen," squealed the bigger female, "come out of that bush and wash your hands this minute!"

Meanwhile, Auntie, lips pursed in concentration, squidged on and on with her foot. The tiny one watched her for a while.

"What are you doing, Auntie?" she asked, swallowing whole whatever it was that she had been chewing.

"Wasp," replied Auntie grimly. "I'm learning him to get his dirty feet on my lunch."

At this point, Stephen appeared nervously amongst the outermost leaves of the hawthorn bush. The big male made a lunge for him, grabbed him by the wrist and yanked him back to the table. Stephen began to cry.

"Just look at him!" shouted the big male and they all did. "How many times have I told him not to pick things up?"

Nobody seemed to know. But Max got a certain grim satisfaction watching Stephen in the middle of all that noise. That'd teach him to turn up here and steal local animals' food. Particularly when he already had a dinner of his own. Perhaps the big male would bite him. To teach him a lesson.

He could almost taste the old, dead bird in the hawthorn bush and the thought of what he'd missed was making him angry. And when a stoat gets angry it gets nasty. Nothing he could do about it.

"I never touched it," wailed Stephen. "Catherine's telling fibs."

"Yes you did," shouted Catherine. "He licked it," she added, smugly.

The big female got up with surprising speed and dragged the wailing Stephen to the boot of the coughing box, just as it seemed the big one was going to aim a swat at him with his plastic box lid.

"I never. I never. Honest I never!" Stephen spluttered as the big female took out some white leaflike things, which smelt strongly of almost-pine, and smeared them over his face and hands.

"She wanted me to pick it up, but I wouldn't and she's just saying it to get me into trouble with Dad," Stephen wailed on between mouthfuls of white leaf-like, almost-pine thing.

If he's telling the truth, thought Max, that dead bird's still in there.

He knew he didn't have any time to lose. There was no telling how many others around the lay-by had come to the same conclusion. Or who these others were, for that matter. He certainly didn't fancy his chances trying to fight off a couple of adult crows in that hawthorn thicket. Even if he was a lot quicker on the ground.

He backed silently out of his burdock clump and bounded along through the tall, coarse grass, bordering the hedge leading over to the bush. Although he was nearing the hawthorn, he still couldn't pick up anything like the unmistakable scent of rotting bird. He was exposed and with no guarantee of a meal at the end of it. But having taken the chance, he had to play it out to its end.

He was moving fast, now. The black tip of his tail pointing sharply back towards Ted's log. Ted of course had the good manners not to inquire where Max was off to. Nosy questions like that were bad for anybody's health and future prospects.

"Get that spray out, Mother." Max heard the big male's angry demand. "Give it over here."

"You can't spray it near food," replied the other one. "It's not safe on food."

"I'd rather eat that than a wasp," shouted the big male. "Now are you going to hand it over or are we going to pack it in here and move on?"

"Well, mind you don't squirt the sandwiches," said the smaller big one. And at that moment Max entered the dark shelter of the hawthorn bush.

He knew where it was the moment he entered the welcome darkness. His nose brought him straight to it. A middle size wood pigeon, torn up by something bigger than he was – could be a cat, maybe even a fox – and played with for a while, then either abandoned or stashed away for a nibble later.

It was enough for dinner anyway. Not as fresh as it could be, but not as old as the tiny ones out there were making out. Max bit into the carcass and shook it, to dislodge the larger insects. Then keeping a lookout for the pigeon's previous owner, he began to tug away at the plump breast.

At the picnic the big male had the spray in his hand. While Auntie and the tiny one kept their hands over the food, he discharged a long arc of poison into the air. Waldo reeled back instinctively but Keef and Stu couldn't control their turns and were carried into the gas cloud by the sheer speed of their flight.

"Clear the area, clear the area," coughed Keef as he hit a blinding wall of liquid poison. "They're gassing us."

Waldo held a holding pattern above the big male's head long enough for his sensors to detect the merest hint of chemical death swirling around in the air.

"Darren, Martin. Regroup, regroup. Follow me. Now!" he snarled, his voice hoarse from the pollution, and then, born to command, he led his flight back to the rotting food box.

Keef and Stu lurched blindly through the picnic killing ground, their tortured muscles driving their wings at twice normal working speed, their little airframes close to breaking apart. They both kept up a frantic buzzing, higher and higher, as they sought to control their wracked bodies.

"Can't see, can't see." Stu crash-landed and scrambled frantically along the table surface, trying to crawl under the lip of a plastic plate away from the suddenly unbearable brightness of the afternoon sunshine. "Waldo? Waldo, where are you? What do I do now?"

He squeezed himself under the plate, his legs working without his brain now, easing himself into the nearest place of quiet and calm. But then suddenly his whole shelter was lifted off him, and he was dazzled in the burning light again.

"Got you!" Catherine brought the jam pot down upon him, crushing and twisting, and the light went out.

"Not with the jam pot, you idiot!" shouted the big male. "Your Mum'll have to clean it off now."

Keef flew blindly away from the noise, faster and faster to escape the pain, with frantic twists and turns as some of his muscles misfired. "Waldo!" he shouted. "Help me! I'll break up if I keep going like this."

Suddenly he found himself over the rotting food box and, squinting through the pain, he thought he could recognise the familiar airborne shapes of his squadron holding formation. Lungs bursting, he tried to steady himself and veer towards them but somehow they seemed to move aside.

"Let him go," hissed Waldo. "He's finished now."

"Waldo?" Keef tried to turn back to the sound, but he seemed to be flying full tilt in all directions at once. Then it just all came apart. And he wasn't a wasp any more.

Max stopped eating and pulled his head back out of the pigeon's carcass. He was full and there was no sense in stuffing himself. It would only slow him down once he had to leave the shady security of the hawthorn bush. And he couldn't stay there much longer. No telling who else had an interest in the dead bird, or how many of them there were, or how big or how desperate.

It was time to go back to his burrow for a little digestive sleep. As he backed quietly out of the hawthorn bush, the lay-by was suddenly filled with enraged shrieks and yells from the unseen picnickers. Max froze to double check he wasn't in view and then loped off along the verge again towards Ted's log.

"Ants, ants everywhere," screamed little Catherine, dropping an anty sandwich back on her plate.

"Ants! Wasps!" bellowed the big male. "The whole place is crawling!"

"Well, let's get off then. I can't eat anything with all the fuss you're making," replied the big female crossly.

So, muttering and snapping at each other, they tried to wipe most of the ants off their picnic equipment before they crammed it all back into the back of little red coughing box.

Then they crammed themselves in the coughing box itself. And started it up. Then they stopped again, and the big female got out and picked up a foot-cover that Stephen had left behind, and then she got back in and they started up again.

Then with the big male shouting at everybody, and Stephen wailing in the back, the little red coughing box pulled tiredly out of the lay-by, with the little boxes still wobbling on its roof.

Max watched it move away up the Roaring Road and then yawned and stretched in the warm summer afternoon. It was definitely time for a sleep.

"Euuh!" Ted made disgusted sounds from under his log. "Euuh! Feuh! Gah!"

"Problem, Ted?" asked Max, drowsily.

Ted put his head out from his log and spat out Keef's mortal remains. "They've done something to this wasp," he complained. "I found it lying just there, all plump and juicy. Bit broken up of course, but you can't have everything."

"Very nice," said Max, absently. He could smell the warm calm of his burrow. The silent safety of underground.

"And you know how I like a good wasp," Ted moaned on. "So I take a good nip at it. And it tastes all hot... well, disgusting and poisonous. Horrible."

"There you go, Ted," Max turned out of his burdock clump and moved off towards the hedge "You taste like that. Bit of a sickener, isn't it?"

He could still hear the toad's spluttering as he sauntered through into the wheatfield and onto the track that would lead him up to one of his current sleeping quarters. The particular bolt hole he had in mind was a vacated bank voles' burrow dug in under the humans' wall that ran alongside the stream leading up to the duckpond.

The burrow was vacated because Max had eaten the occupants and found their shed hair and compressed straw too welcoming to bequeath to any other field rambler. It was the sort of place a bumble bee queen would be only too likely to squat in and build her colony. So he made sure he slept there regularly, to deter intruders.

He didn't make it there though. Something altogether more pressing turned up. Out of the blue June skies. In the shape of a familiar and enticing scent hanging delicately in the air in the bottom corner of the wheatfield, where it met up with the Oak Wood and the Roaring Road cut along beside.

It was a tantalising scent. A feminine scent. The fragrant scent of a young female stoat ready and more than willing to entertain. And it drifted up from the scrubby bracken on the Oak Wood side of the tumbling wall.

Max clambered eagerly through the old stones. His digestion suddenly forgotten along with the sensual diffidence he'd felt and displayed in the past weeks. Like a sudden hunger, physical attraction had raced through him, casting aside any other consideration with its urgent demands. Half way across a field he had discovered desire, or rather desire had fallen upon him like a hawk.

He knew exactly who it was. Claire, the youngest of the females in his area, was warm and waiting nearby. Tucked away underground, in one of the abandoned warrens threading through the scrubland, but near. Very near.

He searched with every sense vibrating and found the entrance almost at once. A burrow near the one he'd escaped to after the night Catherine the owl had nearly killed him. He forced his way down it, impatient, excited and alive.

And there she was. Claire. Healthy, slim and shining eyed. Suckling her young brood, a sinewy male and two lissom females. Max ignored the young male, no threat and probably a grateful recipient of the odd vole's head, should he stick around.

It was the girls and their mother that entranced him. They looked over with a soft-eyed welcome, and snuggled together to give him more room. But Max held back and cautiously sniffed the chamber walls around them.

"Their dad's long gone." Claire had just a teasing hint of mockery in her voice, a challenge to his self-esteem. "Other side of the Pig Killers he is. These days."

"Big Dave, was it?" The reek still lingered faintly in the earth.

She stretched languidly and smiled and Max knew the father of the litter was indeed Big Dave, a prodigious fighter and breeder. Big Dave was the kind of stoat Max had to

grow into, if life allowed him the time, the luck and the space to do it.

But Max wasn't going to give him credit for all that here. He threw Claire a shrug that looked suitably unimpressed by the bigger male.

"Could come back any time. Of course." She smiled up at him. "See the family. Start another."

Max nuzzled lightly at the young. They smelled fresh and milky with a musky warmth like a light summer's breeze through the wheat. He looked over them, as they suckled, towards Claire's sloping, smiling eyes. Why was she warning him off?

"So you better hurry up, then. Hadn't you?" And she gave him a mischievous grin and shifted around in the straw packed chamber to let him get very, very close to her.

At that moment, Max possessed all a stoat could want. He was safe, he was fed and a healthy, young female was offering herself to him. He threw himself into the moment.

"What's that horrible taste on your fur?" she complained, trying unsuccessfully to pull away.

"A bit of human squirty." Max snapped impatiently. "There were some wasps and this spray stuff. And… look!" he rose up, "Does it matter?"

She gave the fur on his chest a placatory groom, "Not very nice. Spect it'll go, though."

"Ted ate some. And he's alright."

"Who's Ted?"

"Oh, never mind."

She laughed at his truculence and his earnest determination. At the same time she knew she was the sole focus of his need and that knowledge grew within her and captivated her. And so, she laughed at his exasperation and then forgot all about Ted and the wasps and the humans and thought only of being there with him.

And the remaining traces of human squirty stuff faded away as the burrow filled with the warmth of life rekindling itself against the imminent dangers of tomorrow.

# July

## Keeping Death off the Road

A warm, drowsy summer's night. Max crouched in the stubby grass as near to the kerbside as he dared. His only refuge was a bedraggled and rather oily clump of cow parsley, holding its own just a few feet away.

He was watching Harry the hedgehog who was squatting contentedly in the middle of the hard shoulder, the half-moonlight glinting on the points of his prickles.

"Nothing like a still night," said Harry happily, throwing the summer moon an appreciative glance. "It catches them lovely on a still night."

"You're the expert," said Max, very unsure of his ground.

As he spoke, two malignant yellow eyes suddenly appeared from around the bend just down the road, poisoning the darkness, and a massive, roaring hulk of heart-stopping power hurled itself upon them.

At once the black mass engulfed them in its noise and

smell, paralysing their senses. Then there was a second of pure stillness, followed by a deluge of filth and the shattered bodies of impacted moths and other free-flying night insects.

"Party time!" yelled Harry, and he trundled cheerily out into the Roaring Road to join in the festivities. Max kept his belly close to the damp grass, the terrifying shockwaves of the monster still reverberating through him.

"I can't see why they don't keep them all for themselves," chortled Harry, as he scurried around busily in his hedgehog heaven. "But I'm not complaining." Then, rather indistinctly with a mouthful of fragmented moth, "Come on, Max, have as many as you like. There'll be another one along in a minute."

And there was. And another and another. And Harry kept eating and chuckling, and Max felt more and more exposed. Almost overcome by the juddering danger of the massive beasts that showered the midnight verges with dead and mutilated insects.

Even so, with all the thunderous crashing of the night traffic, Max's feet detected the threat beneath him at once.

He pivoted around on his back legs to confront the precise point of the danger welling up from beneath him, teeth bared in first-strike fury, weight balanced on his back legs for merciless assault or headlong flight.

The soil suddenly erupted in front of his nose and, as it broke, a smell flooded out through the breach that relaxed him immediately.

Kevin's sun starved, sickly features squinted towards him.

"That's you, Max, isn't it?" said Kevin with his unmistakable whine, half-holding his breath as his snout foraged out in to the world. "I never forget a reek."

"Evening, Kevin," replied Max, guardedly. "You gave me quite a shock turning up like that. Can't you give a bit of warning?"

"Not if I want to stay alive and worming, no." The mole waggled his pink but powerful front paws at the night.

"Never know who you're going to run into do you? Want to talk worms?"

"Talk what?" Max was puzzled.

"Worms. Worms. Worms. Worms. Worms. Worms." Kevin suddenly gave vent to a breathless, excited chant.

"What are you…?"

"Just making polite conversation. Worms. Worms. Worms. Worms. Worms."

Harry looked over from the last of his current batch of fast food moths. "He's being sociable," he explained. "It's the only thing he knows or cares about."

"Worms, worms, worms. Big fat worms," breathed Kevin fast and furiously.

"Pretty soon he'll feel he's had enough surface contact," continued Harry, "and then he'll push off back down there again."

"He's not making much of an effort, is he?" said Max, edgily. "I think he's trying something on."

"Small, wiggly worms. Huge, juicy worms. Cut in half. Wiggling in both directions." Kevin's voice rose ecstatically.

"I'm sorry, Harry," Max's voice was just a lethal whisper in the night, "but I'm going to have to bite his head off. He's getting on my nerves."

"You'll never make it," replied Harry, good-naturedly. "Little beggar's far too quick. Come and have some moths with me. I've found some really juicy ones."

Max weighed up the alternatives – Kevin's head or a couple of moths – and in that instant the mole disappeared, leaving just the foetid breath of underground hovering around his mole-hill, while down below he scuttled along his tight-fitting worm runs, snuffling blindly but acutely for another wriggling mouthful of the love of his life.

Still, even though Mole's Head was now off the menu, Max really couldn't work up a healthy appetite for the stubby, fractured insects jerking out their last conscious moments on the greasy tarmac.

"How's your boy, Harry?" he asked the chomping hedgehog, in a vain attempt to change the subject.

"Lazy, little prickle!" snorted Harry. "He's found himself a milk pool in some human flower-field. Cliff won't bother himself coming down here for a decent meal."

"Hanging round them, is he?" Max sucked air in through his razor teeth. "Too risky for me."

"And you're a throat-biting, blood-sucking stoat, with all due respect!" cried Harry, suddenly overwhelmed by a rare burst of paternal emotion. "If I've told him once, I've told him a hundred times! There's no such thing in this world as an easy meal, Cliff! Except down here with the moths!"

"I get edgy just watching them across the other side of a field." Max tensed involuntarily at the thought of those dangerous, noisy pinkish beings that brought death from directions you'd never even thought existed. "But going right into their flower-fields, near their burrows and stealing their milk. I'd say that was suicidal."

"I've told him. I've said you don't get stoats or badgers or the rest of the Blood and Guts Crew within ten miles of those places, what makes you think you're such a hard-case? Nothing personal, Max."

"That's alright, Harry, I can see you're upset."

"Can you?"

"You just missed a really big brown hairy one behind you."

"Where?" With a surprising burst of speed, Harry whipped round and scuttled back to it. A few moments passed while he chewed vigorously and then, "Kids! You wouldn't credit 'em, would you? Do you know what he says to me?"

"What's he say to you, then, Harry?" Max tried to hide quite how boring the conversation was becoming to him, as the hunger pangs pressed their urgent claim.

"He says if the place is stiff with mice and voles and little bunnies in special boxes, and weenie little ponds full of happy fish, he can't see what there is to be afraid of."

Max stood up on his back legs and looked at Harry with new interest. "Did you say mice?"

"Mice and voles all over the place at night, Cliff says. Reckons the lights are too bright to bring the owls in. Reckons it's a regular mouse carnival down there."

Max's nostrils quivered. It had been an empty night so far. Very, very empty. That was what had brought him to Harry's stretch of roadway. But now the thought of a few plump, complacent mice put Harry's moth banquet in a completely different perspective.

"I told him, Max. I said, 'Cliff, my son, if those mice are up there, it's because those humans are too busy eating hedgehogs to bother with them.'"

Max thought over the risks. Cliff was hardly a wild-fanged fury. If a mud-snuffling trundler like him could move in and out of human flower-fields unscathed, surely he, Max, one of the slickest of the Blood and Guts Crew as Harry so vividly put it, would have no problem picking himself up a mouse supper.

Or was that just his hunger talking? He focussed harder on the tactical problems. He knew he had to ignore his stomach if he wanted to be still around to fill it tomorrow.

A little search and destroy wasn't out of the question, though. He knew his way round the Pig Killers, after all. And he'd made frequent raids around the duckpond and the humans' green patch. Moving a little further into the burrows beyond the green wouldn't do any harm. Get in close, have a look round, and if he didn't like it, get out quick. Little bunnies in boxes, Harry had said. That clinched it.

"I think I'll be moving on, Harry. Got a little bit of business waiting." Max dropped back onto all four feet and checked the short distance between him and the relative shelter of the longer grass up the verge.

Harry was speechless with moth and amazement. Finally he managed to blurt, "What about your dinner?"

"More for you, eh?" said Max backing off politely but firmly.

"There's plenty for everybody," protested Harry. "Look! Here comes another."

Another pair of poisonous yellow eyes flared round the bend and as Max reached the long grass, he felt the windrush of the monster as it passed and heard, over the stinking roar, Harry's whoops of jubilation.

He loped steadily along the upper slopes of the verge, keeping close to the stubbly thorn hedgerow that interceded between the Roaring Road and the wheatfield and the meadows beyond.

There in the wheatfield, if you were very lucky and even quicker, you could jump up and snatch tiny harvest mice off the wheat-ears like soft meatballs on sticks. Trouble was, all that jumping didn't seem to match up to the amount of food you got out off the little squeaking fur-bundles. Sometimes you went home even hungrier than you went out.

Now, well fed field mice were a different proposition altogether. They bustled around finding stores of grain or fruit or seeds and then obligingly filled themselves into roly-poly parcels. Very satisfying. Usually Max just left the ears and feet. Never any real flavour to them.

Of course, he really preferred a good water rat. They often took a little more trouble but it was definitely worth it. Water rats were his weakness, if he had one. And if he had a weakness it hadn't killed him yet.

All at once he was at the hedge-break that led to the rabbit run across the next meadow. At the little well worn hole (this was a major traffic intersection) where the mud was stamped hard and flat by countless different feet, claws and pads – was a human's foot cover.

There was still some human smell to it, although it was wet and dank now after all this time in the open air. Max gave it the once over – you could never be sure – but there was nobody inside it tonight. Well, a couple of woodlice tried to squirm back under its rotting sole as he turned it over with his nose but Max had field mice on his mind, and left them to it.

He knew where he had to make for. Cliff was a steady mover but he was no explorer, so his favourite flower-fields were well within Max's foraging range. Four of them lay side by side, behind the human burrows planted at the side of a little lane leading up to the green patch and the duckpond. The lane joined the Roaring Road just a short distance past the lay-by and the burrows were planted a good run down it, where the Hazel Coppice began.

He'd follow the hedgerow past the wheatfield to where it joined the meadow and cut in by the rabbit run. If he kept to that he could move safely through the coarse grass, cross the lane opposite the Hazel Coppice and edge back towards the trees right next to the flower-fields. Once there, he'd prepare for his final move into enemy territory.

The moonlight was against him, of course. Perfect sighting conditions like that made him a gift for owls. Not much he could do about that; he'd be working blind out there. And the memory of Catherine the owl and the shrieking impact of the talons into his back made him shiver.

He'd got away once, almost unheard of, even for a member of the Blood and Guts Crew. And he knew the safety drill, the Last Resort Tactic of drawing a dive-bombing bird's attention away at the final moment by whisking your tail. But it was risky with owls.

It might work with a kestrel during the day – he knew animals alive because of it – but the murderous precision of an owl wasn't easily diverted. He'd just have to keep in the long grass at the side of the run and hope the owls were having a good run of luck with the field mice.

He'd have to hope his luck was holding out.

He'd gone barely twenty yards along the meandering run when his nighttime's itinerary changed completely. And he knew that luck was with him.

Keening around the next gorse-edged bend Max heard the unmistakable and entrancing noise of blinding, desperate panic. Only inches away a rabbit was in horrifying trouble.

Max darted quicksilver fast through the gorse, homing in on the squealing and the drumming of thrashing, clubbing feet. He was upon her in seconds. The best news he'd had all day. The perfect reason for not risking death or worse in some human's flower field.

A young female rabbit was caught in a human's wire snare. The trap had clearly been set for a heavier buck rabbit, maybe even a hare, for the doe's momentum had carried her head and front shoulders cleanly through the wire noose, which now held her tightly around the waist, cutting in deeper and deeper as she struggled frantically to escape.

The moment she saw Max all struggles ceased. She lay still and rested her head upon the impacted grass beneath her. Exhausted by her desperation and numbed by the inevitability of violent death, she watched Max with a kind of dazed curiosity. Nothing really mattered now.

Max moved forward slowly, scenting carefully to see if the snare setter was close by, perhaps with his dog. But the only reek on the night air was Max's own, and the sweet smell of a rabbit beyond the need for hope.

She shifted hesitantly as Max slipped up behind her head and placed his front feet on her back. His feet rose and fell as she breathed softly beneath him.

"Dear oh dear oh dear," Max whispered gently in her ear. "This really isn't your day, is it?"

And then, with one final glance over his shoulder for the human snare setter, Max fell upon her neck and tore the life from her.

It wasn't a meal to enjoy. He couldn't drag the carcass into any cover so he ate in a frantic hurry, half expecting at any moment an owl to focus in on him or a dog to tumble him over. But soon he was full and, wiping the blood from his eyes, he ducked back into the gorse. Now all he needed was somewhere to rest and digest.

He'd only gone a few feet further, when he could smell the rabbit again, and this worried him. It was her living scent, altogether different from the heady aroma of her blood and flesh that still filled his nostrils.

A few feet further still and he found out why. There was a burrow entrance right beside the run, half-collapsed and impassable but filled with her presence. The fresh blockage may have been what sent her back out into the wire noose, but it made life a lot safer for Max, and he settled down to rest.

He slept well and deeply. But not too deep to keep on sleeping when, as ever without warning, someone was coming.

Before he opened his eyes Max had already picked up the approach of steady, stomping footfalls and staccato panting, punctuated with little snorts of anger and exasperation.

On full alert he stabbed his head to the end of the burrow's entrance, just short of the overhanging grass, and waited to repel whatever ravenous assault something was going to hurl upon him.

Harry's son Cliff trundled past, his prickles rustling and scratching against the coarse grass on the side of the rabbit run. He was muttering short angry hedgehog phrases to himself, digging his claws into the impacted mud to emphasise one bad-tempered point or another.

"Cliff?" said Max and that was when he knew the rabbit supper really had made him dozy. Normally he'd never have given his position away.

"What?" snapped Cliff, still engulfed in his vile temper. Then his basic survival instincts shrieked at him and he immediately rolled himself into a spiky ball and crashed into a clump of dandelion beside Max's temporary restroom.

"Who's there?" His voice, more unsettled than moody now, wavered out from the centre of his bristling defence system.

"It's me. Max," said Max, trying to make out which end of the bristles he ought to be talking to.

"Perfect. That's all I need," grouched Cliff. "I don't know why I woke up, today, I really don't."

"I was with your dad before," said Max, convinced he was talking to the wrong end. "I left him on the Roaring Road. I was coming to those flower-fields you go to."

This didn't seem to interest Cliff at all. He kept right on in the same bitter tone as before. "Alright, Max. On the one hand, you can go for it, try and get a bite in while I put a spine through both your eyes. Or, on the other hand, you can sit here like this and wait for that rotten great dog to turn up. What's it going to be?"

"I'm not going to have a go for you, Cliff," Max tried to mask his exasperation. He'd never get anywhere if Cliff took umbrage. And Cliff took umbrage at practically everything. "Why don't you just unwind and tell me about this dog?"

"Nice try, Max," said Cliff, remaining in his ball, "but I wasn't born yesterday."

Max moved up close to the ball. He had to find out about that dog and quickly. Then inspiration struck. "You're perfectly safe, Cliff. I've just had a rabbit supper and I can prove it. Breathe in."

Max stood up and filed his lungs with warm summer night air. Then he dropped back onto all fours and exhaled deeply as close as he could to the prickles he believed ought to be hiding Cliff's nose. He didn't seem to be far off. With an uncharacteristically high-pitched wail, Cliff unrolled in disgust.

"For crying out loud, Max, you haven't been eating rabbit, you've been gargling it."

"Come on. We've got to keep moving," Max set off briskly. "You can tell me about the dog as we go."

Rounding the bend as they moved back down the run towards the lay-by, Cliff snuffled through those remains of Max's dinner still partially attached to the snare. The young hedgehog's nose wrinkled. "How many of you were there?" he shuddered.

"Just me," said Max impatiently. "Dog, Cliff. What about the dog?"

"There's a new one down there. Size of a sheep. Vicious

like a badger." Just talking about it gave Cliff a fresh burst of speed. Max moved into a higher gear to keep alongside.

"One minute I've got me snout in the milk pool, next minute he's rolling me all over the flower-field. Up and down. Here and there. Up and down again. Wouldn't leave it alone." Cliff scurried on, the memory a fresh wound upon him. Then, "That's not you laughing is it, Max?"

"Not me, Cliff," said Max hurriedly. "I just can't work it out. He's got all those rabbits down there, right?"

"Right," agreed Cliff, highly aggrieved. "In little boxes, going nowhere. Why's he want to eat me?"

Max paused and turned, standing on his hind legs. He closed his eyes and scented acutely. Then he strained his ears in the still night. A faraway owl, a stirring vole, a hare speeding through the wheat in the distance. But, try as he might, he just couldn't pick up any trace of dogness behind them.

"He's not right in the head," Cliff answered his own question,

"That's why he wants to eat me when there's little rabbits going begging. What can you do with something that's not right in the head, Max? What precautions can you take for the out and out nutter?"

Max settled back on his forefeet. "He's not coming, Cliff. There's no dog in this field."

"Must have lost him." Cliff made it sound a dismal victory.

"Taken best part of the night, just to stay hungry."

"Your Dad's down the road, remember?" suggested Max. "I'm sure he'd be glad of the company."

"No thanks. I can't face him and his moths after a night like I've had," said Cliff. "I think I'll go down the lay-by. See if the humans have let anything fall out of the rotting food box."

Max watched him trundle off. And then the mention of the rotting food box reminded him of mice and, although he was stuffed full, he thought he might have a wander down himself. He could probably fit one in. As a treat.

So he caught up with the hedgehog and they walked down the run to the lay-by together. And dawn broke busily all around them. Which meant that Max knew the lay-by was probably going to be a disappointment.

Nothing much would be going on there while the day shift changed over with the night shift; the birds making all their racket as the last of the nocturnals tucked themselves wearily away for some daytime respite. Even those who worked both shifts would be trying to find their bearings as the pale sunlight threatened to expose them to new and varied dangers. Nothing worth eating would be off its guard enough yet.

Max sat in his clump of burdock, on the outside chance that a mouse might start sleepwalking, while Cliff rummaged noisily in a discarded plastic bag by the rotting food box. So Max was first to notice when Brian and Ray, the crow brothers, showed up.

They landed light on their feet – their bulky, lethal bodyweight evenly balanced and poised for an explosion of deranged cruelty at any moment – and then strutted with complete assurance over to Max.

Brian, as ever, led the way, his cold eyes sweeping the lay-by with amused disdain, his plumage immaculate. Ray brought up the rear in shaky, erratic darts, peering out at the world in perpetual challenge. Fear was a stranger to Ray. Along with sanity.

Max said nothing. Whatever the crows had in mind, they'd get round to it in their own time. His best chance lay in fast response.

Brian waited for Ray to stand shoulder to shoulder with him and then turned his head towards Max in the burdock patch.

Max made sure his weight was distributed properly for the attack. And he made sure the crows didn't notice.

"What you got in the bag, Max?" Brian jabbed with his beak towards Cliff's hidden fumblings in the shiny holding thing.

"Nothing to do with me," said Max. Why die for a hedgehog?

"It's Cliff. The hedgehog. Harry's boy."

"There's a stroke of luck," said Brian with satisfaction, and he stared at Max fixedly as if he expected him to share the opinion.

"There's a stroke of luck," agreed Ray and he tossed a bottle top up from the gutter to celebrate, forgetting it the moment it flew into the air. "We come looking for him."

"Tell him to come out, will you Max?" asked Brian softly. "Say we need a word. Family matter."

"Family matter alright," said Ray suddenly moving close in to Cliff's plastic bag.

"Why can't you tell him, Brian?" Max tried not to show his teeth. Fear or aggression could get things moving far too fast here.

"Because I'll frighten him," demonstrated Brian with a chilling patience in his tone. "Won't I, Max?"

Max called across to Cliff in the bag. He wasn't about to wander out of his burdock clump. "Cliff can you come out of the bag? Brian and Ray want a word."

Cliff's breathy rustlings stopped at once. The bag froze. Brian looked reproachfully at Max. Max didn't need the aggravation so he kept on with the job.

"If you don't come out, they're likely to drag you out, Cliff," Max continued, and then slightly brighter, "they say it's a family matter."

"Good boy." Brian nodded to Max, as Cliff nosed his way out of the bag for his family matter.

Both crows stared silently down at him, until he had completely emerged into the morning sunlight. Then Brian, as ever, started the ball rolling. "Hello, Cliffy. How's it going?"

"Mustn't grumble," replied Cliff throatily, his eyes weren't quite open, his back left foot scuffed in the dust in a rhythm all of its own.

"I'm afraid we've got some bad news for you, Cliffy," Brian's voice was gentle, almost hypnotic, "about your Dad."

"He's dead. We just cleaned him up," said Ray abruptly.

He jerked his head forward for no discernible reason and then focussed on an empty jam-jar behind Cliff's quivering form. "That's got a dead wasp on it, that has," he said accusingly.

"We didn't want you to hear it from strangers," Brian continued softly. "So we come down to pay our respects."

Cliff stared at the ground before him. His prickles seemed to droop. He stretched his neck as if it were paining him, but he couldn't seem to find the next set of words.

"How did it happen?" Max had seen the hedgehog's eyes widen and brim with tears. It made him angry. And anger made him reckless. "What happened to him, Brian?"

"Life in the fast lane, I'm afraid, Max." Brian nodded all too wisely.

"He was spread over most of the fast lane when we found him," added Ray.

It had taken some time for Cliff to get to grips with it." You've eaten my Dad."

"We just give him a good send off," said Ray.

"It's the way he'd have wanted it," Brian assured the snuffling hedgehog. "You got to think of his dignity."

"He wouldn't have wanted to be smeared all over the neighbourhood," argued Ray. "What kind of a way is that for your friends to remember you?"

Cliff remained silent for a while. Then he looked up at the two large black birds, the two glistening black beaks. "I understand," he said very softly. "Thank you."

"Think nothing of it," said Brian. "What are friends for?" And with a sudden violent snap he was airborne, shooting away from them further down the Roaring Road.

Ray was just a heartbeat behind him but wheeled on some impulse and returned to fly over the stranded Cliff and the ducking, snarling Max.

"Be lucky!" shouted Ray formally, and then he turned and sped after his brother already a disappearing dot in the new morning sunlight.

# August

## The Harvest Festival

The day was going to be a hot one. Not a breeze stirred the air, still apart from the hum of the bees and the hoverflies in the fields beyond the embankment.

By rights the days should be cooling; the cow wheat was already flowering in the shade at the wood's edge. But today the sun just wasn't following the plan. It beat through the feathery bracts of wild carrot and the button flowered tansy to lie heavy on Max's back as he coursed the hedgerow separating field from roadside and wheat from oily grass.

Tansy fringed the lay-by and its lemon scent masked all trace of the rotting food box. Which meant it could be masking other things. Hungry things with teeth.

So, lunch was not going to be easy. Not that it ever was. But today had added disadvantages. The heat would slow him down. Sap his strength. Cloud his judgement.

Max slipped into his burdock patch, which was now putting out little lilac flowers that somehow smelled of coughing boxes. He pushed his head clear to scan the lay-by and its opportunities.

It all looked still and empty. He gave the place a second slow visual sweep. Empty. Impossibly empty.

It was the shadow that handed Max back his life. The shadow he picked up in the dust by his nose the moment it crashed down upon him. Which was half a second before the hawk's outstretched talons snatched at his back.

Max instinctively rolled one way and whisked the black tip of his tail the other. The hawk's peripheral vision caught the tail movement and he tried checking his flight to compensate. But it was too late and he landed heavily in the dust, wings flashing, heart pounding.

Back in the burdock, Max flipped onto all fours and poised himself to launch a counter attack as the bird righted itself desperately. Teeth bared, he watched for the talons, the slashing beak. He saw dust, brown feathers. Heard air being gasped, claws scrabbling, muscles stretching. Then as fast as it had arrived the bird was gone.

"No.No.No.No.No." A pained voice floated down. "Oliver, what have I told you about the sun?"

"He just rolled out of it, Dad. Must have been my downdraft."

"Tell him, Naomi." The pained voice continued and Max finally picked up the adult kestrel hovering high above the lay-by. Two young, a male and a female, flanked it. And a third, male, was climbing back up to join him.

He'd missed them. Worse, he'd almost been taken by a baby. Relief conflicted with anger. But only for a moment. Either feeling could get him killed.

The young female quoted smugly, "Sun means shadows. Shadows mean missed opportunities."

"I almost took a stoat, Dad!" Oliver rejoined formation.

"Stoat? If your mother...." His father dropped the languid drawl momentarily, then, "Is that you, Max?"

Max froze, belly low against the hard earth, and heart

pounding. He snarled in silence.

"You're in the burdock, Max," said the kestrel with boundless condescension. "We can all see you."

"That'll be you, then, Derwent." Max kept still. They had the sky for an observation point and eyesight that could count his eyelashes. "Causing a commotion."

"Sorry about that." Derwent circled lazily, his brood falling in line behind. "Just taking the kids out for a training session."

"Don't let me hold up the family outing."

"This is Naomi and Richard," Derwent dipped a wing in their direction, "and you've met Oliver."

"He almost lost it, Derwent." Max tried to float a warning into the paternal side of Derwent's predatory nature.

"Not so sure, Max," Derwent remarked dryly. "If you asked me, I'd say you were very, very lucky just then."

"Have it your way." Max kept to the burdock's centre. "Still. Bit of a gamble on a youngster's first outing."

"Never do what you tell them," Derwent conceded ruefully,

"wait till you've got your own."

"I nearly got you," protested Oliver, "and I will next time. Fact..." and he dropped into a dive position.

"If you're old enough to leave formation, Oliver," Derwent's voice cut through the air, "you're old enough to leave home."

Oliver drew up, gave a couple of bad tempered flaps of his wings and then flew in an infuriatingly slow arc to rejoin his family group. Derwent didn't rise to it. He called down to Max as the only other adult there.

"Complete waste of energy, anyway. The humans are unleashing a fieldeater not even a glide away." The kestrel drifted out a few reassuring feet, "Be rabbits, voles, and mice all over the show. Once that gets going." Then he confided socially in Max, "I told Marion I'd take this lot off for a practice. While it's simple."

Like eggs in a nest, thought Max, but he kept it to

himself. He didn't believe a word of it. "Give it up, Derwent. Humans have got all their burrows by the duckpond. They won't let a fieldeater loose near them. Nobody's that stupid."

"Well we can see it from here, Mr Bum-in-the-Mud!" shouted Oliver. "So who's stupid, now?"

"Oliver. That's enough."

"He doesn't believe you, Dad."

"He's just seen what a fieldeater does. Eh, Max?"

"It's a big thing," said Emily. "Just sitting there in that wheatfield."

"With humans all round it," Richard added, with a morbid interest. "Hurry up, Dad. I want to see one up close."

"It's there alright, Max," called Derwent. "Not so far from their burrows, I grant you. But they don't seem that exercised by it."

"Madness. Leaving your brood near one of those things."

"Maybe they know how much it can eat at one go." Derwent completed his final circle of the lay-by. "Anyway, make of that what you will. We're off for lunch. Come on brats."

"Thanks, Derwent. I might be over later."

The kestrel dipped his wings in salute and led his brood away towards the wheat. He called over his wing. "Apologies once again."

"Boys will be boys." Max could afford to be charitable, now they were leaving.

If Derwent's fieldeater was gathering up its strength and its monstrous appetite barely a field's width away there was a definite opportunity here.

The moment the humans unleashed its awful destructive power, it would set off a stampede of terrified field dwellers. Desperate refugees would come hurtling down every path leading out of and alongside the field. They'd launch themselves through every boundary fissure, with a horror-struck determination to get away and no thought of the consequences.

Now he, Max, could easily be one of those consequences. All he had to do was pick his spot and wait. For rabbits, voles, fieldmice, dormice, and rats, hares, maybe baby partridges and pheasants – the menu was endless and running straight into your bite.

So much for the good news. Max stopped tasting rabbit, and started facing facts. Every meal had a price tag. And with a fieldeater, the risks were almost suicidal.

The monster devoured everything in its path, wheat, flowers, birds – nests and all – and of course – rabbits, voles, fieldmice, dormice, rats, hares, partridges, pheasants and anything that could serve as lunch. And it didn't stop there. It ate foxes, hedgehogs, and hawks if they were too slow diving away.

It snatched them all up in its colossal mouth, crushing and pulping them, digested them in seconds and then excreted them in spoor like monstrous owl pellets.

It left behind it a devastated landscape, reeking of the stench of oily, with torn shreds of wheat pointing at the sky and scattered dung-hulks of smashed wheat and shredded flowers close-packed round smothered bodies of the dead and the maimed, hunted and hunter alike.

The humans would drag these hulks of dung away to one of their big burrows, like a butcher bird hoards rotting flesh. Then, their killing fever unabated, they'd return to put flames to the chopped stalks. It was as if they wanted to kill the soil itself, and the stones beneath it.

Given all the pandemonium, snatching lunch around the fieldeater's attack would be easy. Getting in and out alive would be a different matter.

He'd have to cut through the hedge behind him and follow the animal track that ran back away from the Roaring Road alongside the fence of sharp and shiny that separated the wheatfield from the hayfield.

At the far end of the track the field ended and there was a hawthorn hedge and, beyond that, a lane leading down to the duckpond and the human burrows and their little flower-fields. Just the other side of that lane was a large chestnut tree in the middle of the Hazel Coppice.

If he could get into some cover that end of the track, he could pick off a running rabbit or two and, if the fieldeater turned on him, he could dart through the hawthorn hedge, risk the lane and dive into the hazels around the chestnut tree. He had never seen a fieldeater trying to take on a tree. So it should be a safe area.

It wasn't much of a plan. But it was the only one he had. And the hunger was gnawing at him to make the most of it.

৪৯

Mona let the thermals drift her above the wheat stalks towards the tangle of brambles, old sharp and shiny and rotted wood slats that squatted in a confused heap at the corner of the wheat field.

Whatever the humans had used it for before, it was long abandoned to brambles, dry grass and, bliss upon bliss, an unaccountable buddleia whose purple cones drooped over the wreckage.

Brambles and buddleia. Mona reheated, put on a little burst of speed across the sea of wheat and bobbled her way through a sputtering pair of tortoiseshell butterflies.

"Mind out!" she thought. Or perhaps she'd even said it. She'd been at this so long, she'd every reason to talk to herself.

"Oh, very nice," complained the first tortoiseshell, fluttering indecisively above a wheatear as Mona droned her determined way through his flight path. "Just what we need. A buzzing great bumble bee clogging up the air lanes."

"Ignore her, Geoff." His companion landed on the

adjacent ear, and tantalised him by playing with her proboscis. "They get funny at that age."

Geoff watched the display.

"Lisa, you are a very naughty tortoiseshell," he said, more in hope than conviction.

"And you are about to find out," Lisa replied. Then she gave a promissory giggle and fast fluttered back towards the centre of the field.

"Am I? Oh, am I?" asked Geoff delightedly, and he flew off in the hottest pursuit.

Mona hovered above the brambles, bumping her way gently through some hoverflies. Through the heady blend of fresh pollens and nectars, she could detect the long dead echo of old wax, pollen stores and brood clusters. Somebody has set a colony here long ago. Under the rotting wood, no doubt. In a second hand mouse nest, most likely. Hadn't been one of her tribe. Wrong smell altogether. But a bumble nonetheless.

Mona hoped it had prospered. She hoped it had survived the weather, the parasites, the birds, and the colony invaders. She hoped it had produced queens. Big, fat, healthy, young queens stuffed with eggs and nectar.

She just didn't know why.

Mona climbed into one of the purple cones, a little frisson of greed quivering inside her. She landed intoxicated with it but missed her footing and dropped out of the flower.

As she hovered below trying to get her entrance reorganised, she sideswiped into Diane.

"Sorry, dear," said Mona to herself. She didn't know the other bee at all. But she did know she would be as deaf as she was.

"Sorry, dear," replied Diane for form's sake. And the two elderly foragers tried to steer themselves out of each other's space.

From the white tail Mona could tell Diane was from a different tribe altogether. They were more or less equally matched in size. Their hair as worn and tatty, their pollen baskets as well used. Their wings as tired.

We've been around the pollen too long to worry about a buddleia, they thought synchronically. I just hope the poor old bee gets home.

Of course you didn't get that kind of attitude with the slave bees, the industrials. Bees On A Mission they were; flew right through you. Stung you if you were in the way. Feeding the hives, filling their quotas, serving their masters. Bees in bondage.

Anybody who had anything to do with those humans went funny, reflected Mona, shepherding Diane into the next cone up, and then docking carefully into the one she'd selected for herself.

Sunshine penetrated the flower wall. Bathing Mona in purple light. The savour of nectar was pervasive and sublime and the old worker sighed, suffused in quiet content. This stuff was fit for a Queen.

❧

A few feet south of Mona's private exaltation, Max scrambled into the tangle of rotten wood, bramble and old sharp and shiny and sank gratefully into the cool earth beneath. He forced himself to take deep, deliberate breaths – to regulate his breathing and his hammering heartbeat after the long, lung-bursting sprint down the track, away from the Roaring Road.

Peering out through the brambles, he could see the top of the chestnut tree and the hazels shooting up above the nearby hawthorn hedge. They were all still there. And he flinched as the rasping sound of a passing coughing box reminded him that the lane was still there too. He just hoped he didn't have to escape across it.

He could feel his system calming down. The light was

muted down here, the air cool and fragrant. He could hear the soothing sound of bees and other insects buzzing above him. But soothing or not, this was a killing ground even before the fieldeater started up its mayhem.

Most of the flesh eaters would be here already, settling into their ambush points, widening their eyes and checking their focus, compensating for the dazzling sunshine that bounced back off the unusually still field of wheat. If Max showed in their line of sight before a vole did, well they weren't that choosy. They all worked the way he did.

Find it, kill it, eat it and get out fast.

He'd picked this tangle for his ambush point because it lay at the intersection of two main escape routes – the track he'd arrived by and another that snaked back along the lane, in the direction of the duckpond and towards the lurking fieldeater.

Once the fieldeater attacked, the intersection would jam in seconds. A contra-flow of panic, where he could just dart out into the track, pull down a refugee and drag it back under the brambles. He'd take only the lightest targets. The impetus of a buck rabbit in full flight would drag him too far down the killing road before he'd bitten through the base of the skull.

He'd stick with the babies. Maybe store a few up. Although building a larder wasn't really his style. He preferred to eat fresh. And someone could always slither in and feast on your store while you were away or hide behind it all and wait for you. Some malicious farm cat would sprawl for hours behind a pile of uneaten rodents, to work a little mayhem on a smaller, fellow predator.

Well, he'd kill as many as he could as quickly as he could. And work out what to do with them all later.

He pulled round on the defensive at some awkward scurrying in the wheat stalks outside the tangle. Nothing big or heavy boned. And no strung out moves. Just little fits and starts. But too close for all that. He listened acutely. Tried to visualise the source until....

"Frog here."

"Frog here too."

"Frog over here."

Young and hungry, they'd made it out of the pond and were in the fields searching for insects in short tentative forays, occasionally calling out for company. They'd come a long way, for frogs.

In a series of jerks, a lump made unsteady progress under the carpet of wheat fibres and other field mulch that drifted up to the brambles and the tangle. And a tiny wheat coloured frog emerged with a lurch, to lie awkwardly in front of Max's questing nose.

"Frog," it admitted disconsolately.

"You shouldn't be here," said Max disinterestedly. The tiny frog barely breathed. It tried to look away from the stoat. To will itself invisible. "It's going to get very active in a minute. You want to hop off home."

The frog seemed to consider this, subtly redistributing the weight on his feet.

"Frog off," he agreed.

At that, the world began to vibrate and the little frog was bounced repeatedly off the ground as a screeching and roaring erupted, followed by violent threshing and an insistent menacing drumming. The earth reverberated under a furious onslaught.

"Too late, now," Max told the frog and promptly forgot about him, as he took up his position for the stampede.

⁊ꙑ

Already deafened, Max could see almost nothing. The wheatstalks thrashed in a dizzying frenzy. The dust and field mulch whirled up in eddying clouds from the ground.

Two larks came over at wheatear height, shrieking out a

warning. Then a young doe rabbit propelled herself out of the dust and hurtled past Max to crash into the dry grass and dandelion packing the base of the fence behind him. She ricocheted off to the right, caught her balance on the track and without a moment's pause, tore off in the direction of the Roaring Road. Gone in seconds.

The terror had started.

Two more does followed her through Max's blurred vision and into the fence. They split directions, one following the first and the third diving for the hedge and lane. Max crouched ready to spring, trying to predict the next target's trajectory.

A young rat came through, fast and low, and Max went for it, throwing himself up and back as it rushed headlong towards the path. He grabbed its ears for purchase and held on, sinking his teeth into its neck.

Pain and fear kept it forcing a way through and it carried Max out onto the track. Another pair of young rabbits was upon them as Max rolled under the rat to slow it down and keep himself unsighted. Their back legs buffeted him as they jumped over him and turned to spring down the track.

From under the writhing rat, Max watched a brown spectre slash down on the lead rabbit and drag it along the path in clouds of dust to a final fatal impact. Then, with a sharp crack of its wings, the spectre took off into the sun, grasping the inert, bleeding bundle beneath it.

Derwent had started the training session in perfect form.

Max dragged his dead rat back to the vantage point in the tangle. His face was covered in blood from the killer bite but he could still make out some field mice as they streamed past him. He'd wait for a rabbit. Conserve energy. Pull down more flesh per kill. He wiped his eyes, ready to target the next buck or doe out of the frenzy in the field's interior.

"Oi! You've left his 'ead behind." Something had clearly taken umbrage.

"Not only is that a waste. It's also very untidy." A cooler voice chided mockingly.

Max focused fast on two dark shapes poised on a branch of the chestnut tree that inclined into the lane. Brian and Ray, the crow brothers, had turned up early. Normally they arrived once the hard work had been done, to pillage the dying and scavenge the remaining body parts of the dead.

"Why do we always have to clean up after mucky flappers like you?" said Brian with a fatalistic shrug.

"Can't really discuss that now," Max squinted into the wheat dustcloud and the waving corn, feeling for the drumming of footprints under the regular percussive rhythm of the approaching fieldeater. "Got a job on."

"S'not polite that," Ray objected. "S'not good manners."

"Always time for a friend, surely Max," smiled Brian.

Another rabbit colony welled up and broke over Max to dash past to the tracks. He ground his teeth angrily and hunkered back down in launch position, shutting the crows out of his mind.

"My one, dad!" A young kestrel voice. "Watch me."

"Separate targets everybody." Derwent's cool voice floated across the skies. "Pick a target, stick with it, see it through to the death."

"Got the kids out then, Derwent?" rasped Brian. But there was no answer from the focused kestrel.

"Right," Ray pronounced. "I'm having that rat's head."

And with that the killing got properly underway.

Mona found the buddleia trembling about her, the walls of the cone snatching at her wings as it jerked wildly back and forth. She dropped out low in case a bird was hunting through the plant and found herself in the middle of a wheat and dust storm.

She zigzagged blindly through air that pulsated with swirling clouds of chaff, driving herself lower and lower to follow the ground contours out of the field and towards some kind of landmark she could recognise. She thought she caught a glimpse of Diane lying dazed on the ground, but progress was too much of a struggle to focus.

Finally she found herself low against a hawthorn hedge and tacked back and forth up across the surface, rising out of the dust clouds, up the shaded twigs and leaves and into sunshine that started hazy and then grew more intense as she crested the top.

There her wingspeed deserted her, and she sank exhausted into a depression in the leaves just beneath the hedge summit. She was aware of birds, big birds, darting over her and heading into the field. But they weren't moving with the jinking flight of insect eaters. They were banking and plunging, then wheeling up to plunge again.

Being a bee, Mona didn't hear the shrieks of the dying, caught up in the carnage as kestrel and sparrowhawk plundered the escape lanes. Or the hoarse barking of foxes hiding further up the track to snatch up those animals on the brink of safety.

She just felt the disturbance about her and the weight of her pollen fixing her to the leaves. And she waited in the sunshine for her wingspeed to return and take her safely back to the Colony and a job well done.

The sparrowhawk turned expertly in the track and then skimmed the hawthorn hedge, keeping a firm grip on the rabbit it had taken. The rabbit, a baby, was still running, its legs pounding away on automatic pilot. It had only one destination now.

The hawk had landed just inches from Max as he dragged another field mouse back to his cache in the tangle. His stomach had tightened as his deadliest enemy focused itself with chilling precision on another target for the time being. It was enough to bring his own burst of killing to a halt.

He crouched and sniffed at his prey, a rat, a young rabbit still shivering and three fieldmice. More than enough for him, especially with all the dangerous activity outside.

The wheatstorm had abated, the dust dispersed and settled; the refugee stampede had dwindled to a sporadic trickle. The persistent rumble of the fieldeater was receding as it turned back to wreak havoc on the far end of the field, its roars punctuated by occasional cries from its human drovers.

The wheatfield was now partitioned into the destroyed and the yet to be devoured. From time to time cornered animals would take to the open ground, sprinting through the torn stalks. The birds fell upon them. Derwent now flew mute. He'd either said it all before or he was too tired to make the effort.

Richard, Oliver and Naomi grew more and more adroit in slaughter, learning their trade in a time of plenty. Max listened to their breathless banter and then turned his attention to the baby rabbit. He'd eat now. Let the situation calm out there. Then try and drag something back to his burrow for later. For when he woke up.

He bit deep into the rabbit, tearing aside the fur to feast on the liver. He'd worked hard for this. He'd made the kill and he needed fuel and reward. In large bite size chunks.

"Sam!" yelled a human.

"What's the matter with 'im?" said another.

"Must be rabbits!" the first replied. "Drive 'im potty! Sam! Christ sake settle down."

And at that moment Max smelled the dog.

It was a big mongrel and gaining ground. Sniffing and snuffling at the scent of carnage his human masters didn't seem to be picking up. There was blood and death all around and it was disturbing the dog. It reeked of anger and fear.

"Whassat?" It blustered into the tansy lining the fence. Then, receiving no reply, it urinated long and assertively. But it still kept sniffing cautiously, as if death might prove to be a lot bigger than he liked.

Max bit deeper and faster into the guts of the rabbit. If he was scented and he couldn't hide he'd have to move out fast. He needed energy, but not bulk, so he drunk what blood he could, and tore at the remainder of the liver.

"Sam, slow down." The first human was breathless. "Jesus, supposed to be a walk, not a bloody assault course."

"That combine covers some ground. Almost done this field." said his friend.

"Not really Farmer Giles though, is it?" the first

muttered and then, "Hello, he's found something."

The dog had arrived at the tangle. It picked up Max's reek.

"Whassat?" It shouted. "Come on out. Little bleeder!"

Max scampered out the back of the tangle making for the track. Maybe the rat, the mice and what was left of the rabbit would hold the dog off. Keep him busy.

But the dog clearly wasn't hungry. It bounded round the side of the tangle and confronted Max with a snarling rage. "Kill you! Kill! You!"

"Sam! Shut up." The human voice drifted up the track.

"Dead. Barking dead, you are."

Max stared the dog in the eyes. If it had come out of a coughing box, it wouldn't be country fit. It might feel unsettled by a strange animal. It might back off.

"Stoat, is it? Barking stoat!"

Max feinted back into the tangle, drawing the dog with him. It tried to force its bulk through the rotting wood, and the little pile of animal corpses.

"Out. Come on out!" it barked, scrabbling impatiently at the still warm flesh with its forepaws.

As soon as it was fully engaged, thrusting its head and shoulders through two mouldering slats of wood, cross linked in sharp and shiny, Max took his one chance of escape. He streaked from the tangle and headed for the hawthorn hedge.

The dog tried to drag itself back and out, shaking aside wood and obstinate strands of bramble. The humans were almost up to him now.

"Settle down, you daft bugger!" cried the first human.

"Back! Come back! Fight!" the dog bellowed after Max and having pumped up its anger and courage, it hurled itself after him.

Max was through the hawthorn hedge in seconds. He could hear the humans shouting too. Any minute now they might set the fieldeater on him.

He vaulted onto the lane and heard to his horror dog paws skidding on the lane surface behind him. There was a clump of toadflax on the far verge and he launched himself at it.

"Dead! You're dead!" bawled the dog.

Max felt the toadflax close about him, and waited for the dog's jaws to close on him too. But then he was shaken by the bellow of a coughing box followed by an unearthly shriek, a smell of burning and a whine from dog.

"You stupid bloody animal!" shouted a new human.

"Sam. Come here! Come here!" the first human shrieked. And then he spoke softly "Really sorry, mate. Just got away from us."

The humans were all talking at once. The dog slinking away and whining. But Max didn't care what had happened. He just wanted to make it to the heart of the Hazel Coppice, find a dark hole and throw himself into it.

It was a long minute before he found a sanctuary he could trust, but he curled up beneath a root tangle in the coppice centre. Out of sight, and hopefully out of harm's way, he let all the perils of life carry on above without him.

પ્જ

He'd dozed. And then he'd cleaned himself. So that when he emerged, the light was dappled in the Hazel Coppice, the temperature had dropped and the midges were out. The force of the summer sun was, like the dog, long gone. Max pushed his nose from a weed cluster where the Hazel Coppice met the humans' planted grass patch and scented long and hard to make sure.

The dog was long gone. The only sign of human animation was in the highest of the human burrows that stood at the far side of the grass patch. It was the highest burrow, and came to a point in the sky. From within its greyness a regular clanging resonated. Floating around the other burrows, through the Hazel Coppice over the fields.

And around the clanging burrow whirled the swifts. Like sooty meteors, round and round at high speed, the sheer exhilaration of flight causing them to call to each other through their mid-air intersections with effortless precision.

But while their flight was smooth and effortless, their voices shrieked with high tension energy. Cutting through the clanging as they massed for the long journey to the sunsoaked skies of Africa.

"When?"

"Soon!"

"Down and away."

"Soon."

"Over the sea."

"Sun. Hot sun!"

"When?"

"Soon!"

Max watched them darting and turning. It was as if they drew energy from the air and grew it within themselves, to release it in flight. He'd never seen one on the ground. They never stopped. When they left here, they wouldn't stop till they'd crossed the world.

And then, after the icy and snow and dark days and long nights had gone, they'd come back. To start it all again.

Watching them, he realised it was time for him to move on too. Round the humans' grass patch, across the lane and back into the wheatfield. What was left of it. He looked up to check the position of the setting sun and saw, above him, a bumblebee buzzing against the faint breeze.

Mona was keeping her tired bulk in the air mainly through force of habit. She'd lurched off the hawthorn hedge before the cooling air stranded her for the night.

Orientating herself by the straggling rhododendron at the near corner of the human grass patch, she altered her flightpath as directly as her aching muscles would allow, and droned away towards her home in the field of tall stones beside the clanging barrow.

In a far corner of the field of tall stones, behind a small wooden burrow where a human kept oily and bags of nasty and things to cut the grass and gouge the earth, Mona's Queen had discovered the old mouse's nest. There she had brought the colony to life. There she had brought Mona into the world of pollen and nectar and the joyful exhaustion that gathering them incurred.

Mona reheated and pressed on. She was in the home approaches. She could almost taste the sip of honey that was waiting in the colony to welcome her.

A swift took her almost without thinking. It registered a certain sweetness as it bit through her and swallowed her in two fast gulps, and then it looped and banked and rejoined the display.

૪Ꭷ

The dung-hulks cast long shadows across the stubble as Max picked his way carefully across the churned ground. He kept to the pools of darkness that filled the pocks and scars of the plundered earth. His eyes constantly searched the air for a marauder but he knew the chances of an attack were, for the time being, remote.

The hawks would be replete, as would be those owls who had worked the day shift. The latecomers would be waiting for the light to fade when they would sweep the field boundaries for clusters of traumatised mice, looking about them for their next haven now the only home they had known had been pulverised.

The aerobatic exchanges of the swifts as they buzzed the high clanging burrow grew fainter behind him while he crossed the field towards the lay-by. His cache in the tangle belonged to the dog now. What it had not eaten, it would have marked, despoiled for other users. He'd give the rotting food box the once over before he went back to his burrow to celebrate surviving another day with some deep, uninterrupted sleep.

He sped through the shadow cast by one of the monster's dung-hulks and then paused to throw all his attention into his hearing. There was movement deep within it. And once he had focused in on the movement, he heard the muffled voice.

"Oh, Dad. Please Dad." It was a small, exhausted voice. A frightened voice. "Come and get me out, Dad."

Max crept closer to the outer wall of the dung hulk. He could hear listless movements as muscle and sinew struggled fitfully against hard packed wheat. He pushed his head into the crush to sniff out the voice's species. The owner sensed his nearness.

"Who's there?"

"That's Oliver, isn't it?"

"Who's that?"

"What you doing in there, Oliver?"

"I was on the ground, trying this mouse. Just a quick bite, when the monster fell on me and it went dark and hot and crushing and I can't.... Who is that?" fear made Oliver shrill.

"It's me. The stoat. Remember?"

"I nearly had you!" But Oliver's boast was muted by more than just cut wheat.

"That was then," Max spelt it out into the dung-hulk. "This is now."

"Come near me and I'll shred you. Beak your eyes out. Gut you with one claw." Oliver threshed at the wheat bulk that constrained him.

"I'll just wait here, Oliver" explained Max evenly. "You're going to get weaker and weaker. Can't breathe, can you? That's going to get worse. Much worse. And when it does..." the inevitability hung in the air.

"Dad!" Oliver's breathless cry barely reached the wall of the dung-hulk. "I want my Dad."

"He's long gone, Oliver," Max reminded him softly, "and

you're not going anywhere."

Max pulled out a small bed from a softer clump of field poppy snagged into the base of the dung-hulk and curled up comfortably in it. He had all the time in the world.

So, as dusk fell around them, he waited patiently for his next meal to die.

# September

## Stormy Weather

The air hung dense and heavy and the light was somehow muted as the skies loomed over the lay-by. Now and again a huge droplet of rainwater would splatter onto the Roaring Road, a sporadic warning of the storm to come.

In the wheatfield behind the lay-by, the humans were running a muddy coughing box up and down the wheat stubble, dragging something that cut into the earth and turned it raw side up against the browny grey cloud cover. Skylarks and rooks tracked up and down behind it, diving down on the worms and insects the humans exposed with their earthcutter.

Thunder fretted in the distance from across the Roaring Road. Far beyond the Pig Killers' burrows and beyond even the Oak Wood that fringed the pig fields.

Max listened closely as he lay in the hawthorn bush at the end of the lay-by. The hawthorn offered better protection from the coming deluge than his burdock patch.

Beyond the Pig Killers, the pig fields and the Oak Wood was Big Dave's patch. But Max saw no need to venture into it, provided the food held out. Particularly now that he'd mated with one of Big Dave's females over by the Oak Wood. No need to stir up bad feelings unnecessarily. However as he sniffed out the advent of the distant storm, he picked out an intriguing scent flowing in from Big Dave's direction.

It was definitely on his patch, though. Because it was nearer than the dense, dry fug of the pigs up in their shiny arcs in the pig fields at the hillcrest. This scent was nearer and sweeter and welcome.

Rotting apples and plums. Even with the airways paralysed before the downpour, the sickly sweet scent wafted down to Max's quivering nose.

Rotting apples and plums. Just up the lane, the trees in the little fruit tree field by the Pig Killers' burrow were shedding their loads faster than the Pig Killers could gather them. The storms were slowing everybody down. And that meant fruit rotting in sweet juices under the trees, which in turn meant all manner of rats, field mice and voles feeding themselves up for the coming winter.

The real scrabbling hadn't begun yet. There was still plenty of food around to keep the birds busy elsewhere. And the hunters – kestrels, owls, sparrowhawks, and foxes – would be making easy kills in the churned up fields. So the fruit tree field with its sheltering branches and little stone walls would just be the place for safe, steady browsing. There, mice could build up their winter weight, without effort, from fruits that fell before them.

It was ideal. Particularly if you enjoyed the taste of contented, fruit-stuffed rodents. The way Max saw it, if they were picking up an easy meal, why shouldn't he?

Max felt the rising air pressure all around him. The question was, should he launch his raid before or after the storm? If he went now and the storm broke on him, the ditches along the lane up to the fruit tree field would fill with bubbling torrents of water and the mice would scrabble into whatever dry cover they could get to. He could drown getting there, or arrive drenched at a field of useless, sodden fruit without a rodent in sight.

Still, if he waited for the storm to pass, there was no knowing what it might wash away up there. Or indeed how long it would take for the half-drowned mice to return to their foraging. They could stay tucked away, quivering and damp, waiting for the sun to dry out the feeding area. They could stay that way for hours. They'd eaten. He hadn't.

Max watched another few raindrops crash onto the Roaring Road. There were still long intervals between impacts. And the thunder was still muttering and mumbling well away behind the pig stench. He had time to get in and make a start, surely. If he timed it right, he could lie up in the fruit tree field wall, safe above the waterline and digest a couple of voles as the storm waters flooded on by.

The moment the decision was made, Max moved on it. He checked all directions for humans, scoured the skies for a hawk tired of the easy pickings in the wheatfield and then darted across the Roaring Road. He kept low to the cambered surface, trying not to breathe in the oily spoor the coughing boxes smeared everywhere.

In seconds he was up the verge and following the hedge line towards the lane entrance and the ditch that would take him into the Pig Killers' patch and their fruit trees.

Stan the sparrow and his wife Jean watched Max's sprint across the road from a lofty perch on the rim of the rotting food box. Her brother Morris pecked around some crumply white left by the humans at its base. The crumply white had once held wheaty stuff and Morris was hoping to find a few crumbs overlooked by the ants. It was a faint hope, even Morris would acknowledge, but it was something to do before the rains came and swamped everything.

"Wonder where he's going," said Jean as they watched Max disappear into the nettles shrouding the ditch by the lane's entrance. Then she pecked feverishly at a mite nipping her under the left wing pit.

"He's going the other way," Stan observed. "Be thankful for small flapping mercies."

"He's going up the pigs," Jean concluded.

Morris looked up from his invisible crumbs. He quivered for a moment and then loosed a dropping onto the white crumply.

"He'll never take a pig."

Jean looked down to her brother. "What's he going up there for, then?"

"Mayhem. Murder," replied Stan. "Same as wherever he goes."

Jean shook herself, puffed her chest feathers out and sunk her head down between her shoulders. "Doesn't bear thinking about."

"Doesn't bear forgetting either," reminded Stan and with that he dropped down on a chunk of wheaty stuff that Morris had missed behind the white crumply and flew off to the hawthorn bush to finish it.

"I hate the way he does that," complained Morris.

"Quick though, innee?" said Jean, her pride in her partner getting the better of her envy.

🙠

Max kept to the bottom of the ditch. There was no telling who you might meet in there. A vole to snack on before the main business of the day, maybe. But the imminent rain seemed to have pulled everybody out of the hollows and he nosed his way busily through the first of the falling leaves without meeting anybody, friend or food or both.

It was an easier route than the ditches over by the duck-pond near the humans' burrows and the Hazel Coppice. Over there conkers and crab apples tumbled into the sunken runs, bringing small humans in foraging after them.

Whatever other problems he might be running himself into, small noisy humans were thankfully a long way away. The Pig Killers didn't have any young. Just dogs. And only one of those was young enough to be a worry.

He pushed on under the black berries of straggling dogwood bushes, soon to be ravaged by the noisier of the beaked brigades. For now it was quiet. The grass seemed to absorb his footfalls as he pressed deeper into Pig Killer territory. The pig reek hanging warm in the air, ever strengthening in the blend with rotting apples and earth still moist from yesterday's storm.

Everything was warm and damp, even the air. Even the lower stones of the old wall around the fruit tree field. Max sniffed out a cleft hidden behind a shabby nettle patch and then, with a final twisting sprint, he was through the wall and inside the field.

The apple trees loomed over him. Gnarled and twisted over, leaves drooping. The fruit pulped and split amongst the short grass between them. Max set himself between the popping roots of the nearest and scanned the killing ground. All he could see was sticky fruit and tiny motes floating in the dissipating beams of sunlight filtering through the branches.

It was uncanny. No life at all. Until he spotted Waldo at ground level a couple of feet away from him.

"Not really your patch, Waldo," he observed, just to let the wasp know he was there and coming through.

"S'Max innit?" said Waldo walking around in wavering circles on the top of his rotten apple. "Maxie, Maxie, Maxie!" He revved his wings fiercely but lost focus as quickly and stopped.

"What's the problem, Waldo?" Max watched the wasp tilt to one side and then gingerly feel his way down the contour of the apple, until his proboscis disappeared into the dank earth and his abdomen stuck skyward.

"Problem? What stinging problem?" Waldo rasped with sudden venom, staring into the mud. "Ain't got no stinging problem."

Max looked beyond him, searching for tracking moves in the damp grass, tentative mouse runs, quivering and dodging voles. "Terrific," he said absently, and then, "see you around, Waldo."

He continued his wary advance into the fruit tree field and had made a few, cautious feet when the wasp's voice drew him up.

"It's a beautiful world, Max."

"This isn't like you, Waldo." It wasn't.

"It is, mate. A beautiful world. Mainly." Waldo had managed to get back to the top of his apple. He paused and took stock blearily. "Can't see Darren anywhere can you?"

"No." Max scanned the fruit trees till he saw another wasp weaving unsteadily into the pale sunlight around a hot grass box in the field's top corner. A box the Pig Killers kept filling, inexplicably, with old leaves and grass that got hotter and hotter as it sat in there. "Hold on, there's one of your lot over by the hot grass box."

"That'll be Terry," Waldo snorted dismissively, "trying to get back to the nest." He gave his wings a short flex. "Been trying all afternoon. Still a larva half the time, Terry."

"He's doing better than you. Least he's airborne."

"Go anytime I like," protested Waldo. "Just not ready." He thought for a while, "Should get some of this in, Max. Do you a power of good."

"Some of what?"

"Fruity stuff. Don't half make your wings go bendy. Where's Darren? Darren! Max's here!"

"Alright, Max?" A throaty rasp inches away to his left caused Max to throw his weight onto his back legs and push out his bullet head, baring his fangs. "Good here, innit?" continued the voice affably.

Darren was lying on his side in a pool of darkened apple

mulch. He was smeared with it, his wings glued earthbound. He pulled his head out of the viscous mess and gave Max a wobbly grin.

"Been eating that stuff too?"

"Full of it. Old Son. Get it while you can, eh?"

"Get it while you stinging well can!" roared Waldo and he fired himself off his apple to land somewhere behind it.

"No thanks. And you want to watch that," Max said to Darren.

"What happens if you get a bird here? Insect eater. You're in no condition."

"Try me! Stinging well try me!" Waldo's defiance floated out of the grass. Then, "Where you gone, Darren? Darren!"

"We had the farm cat through," Darren said helpfully. "Not long back. I think. So all your little furry friends scuttled up towards…." He tried to nod towards the hot grass box. But couldn't.

"Thanks, Darren." Max couldn't quite believe the helpful attitude.

"Any time, mate."

Any time until the fruity stuff wore off, thought Max. Then he'd be back to being a wasp again. He eased his way past Darren and stalked towards the hot grass box.

"Max?" Waldo voice sniped out again.

"He's gone off," Darren croaked back.

"Typical stinging stoat," Waldo concluded sourly, "never there when you need 'em."

"What'd you ever need a stoat for?" Darren was baffled.

But Waldo was asleep.

§ə

Max crept up beside the hot grass box and listened acutely for the palpitating heartbeats of panic-stricken voles. All he picked up was a weary buzzing above him. Terry was still trying to negotiate the weak thermals over the fruit field wall and home to his wasp nest.

Everything else was still. No birds. No scampering voles. Not even the scuttle of insects. And they were always bustling off somewhere on some secret plan of their own.

Terry sank exhausted onto the top of the wall and staggered into an awkward crouch. Max didn't bother to announce himself. He'd had enough of wasps for the afternoon. They were dangerous and indigestible at the best of times. And this wasn't the best of times.

A few heavy raindrops thudded into the leaf canopy above him. And one managed to break clear through to the fruit carpet beneath. Then stillness regained control.

Then, unpleasantly close, he caught the sound of whispering and a furtive bustling. He stood up and sniffed, straining his ears to pick up the direction of the danger and located it almost immediately. Something was happening deep inside the hot grass box. Inside the grass itself.

The movements were too fluid for mice or voles. The whispering too controlled, but urgent none the less. Max backed off in case some unknown feral threat launched itself at him from its warm vegetal cradle. As he tensed for the attack he picked up sporadic words within the whispers.

"You out?"

"I'm out."

"I'm almost out."

Whatever it was, there was more than one. Gathering together in hushed urgent tones.

"All of us?"

"One more."

"Hot in here."

"Hot. Dark. Safe."

"No food."

"No."

"No food here."

Max stepped back further. There was a pack forming in there under the hot grass. They had to be small. But that was no indicator. He was small compared to a rabbit. And he was deadly.

"And out there?"

"The Wide."

"Yes. The Wide."

"And food."

"All here now."

"It's time."

"Time for the Wide."

This was it. Max knew he'd left it too late to get clean away. If the owners of the voices proved to be a problem, he'd have to fight his way through them to the safety of the wall behind the hot grass box and escape into the meadow beyond.

It could go either way now.

Then in a glistening flurry, a knot of baby grass snakes cascaded out of the base of the hot grass box and slithered onto the flattened ground in front of him. Max danced back as they fanned out sleepily around him, tongues flickering with a questing uncertainty.

There were eight of them, about as long as his body, but thin, new and facing an unknown world. Their voices were light and wispy, almost as if they spoke without words. Just an exchange of beady glances, darting tongues and languorous, scaly shrugs.

"Is this the Wide?"

"Suppose so."

"This way then?"

"Or this."

"Or this."

"What's this here?"

They had stopped in various angles of exit and were staring indirectly at Max. He froze.

"Too big to eat."

"Eat us?"

"Hasn't yet."

One immediately rolled onto its back and played dead. Its green colour blanched to grey and a thin, evil smell emanated from it.

"No point."

"Move on."

"There's more Wide over here."

"And over here."

"There's Wide everywhere."

The rest of the baby snakes started to move off. And Max let them separate and slither off into the wide, new world. Then he darted after the last straggler which had pulled up and was throwing its curious glances around the pulpy floor of the fruit tree field, jabbing its tongue out in darting questions of discovery.

Max pounced on it. He bit deep into the back of the snake's head and then threw it aloft to shake out its last living moments. It wasn't a vole. It wasn't his favourite. But it was here and it was fuel. And if you waited around for your ideal meal, you ended up as someone else's.

The baby snake playing dead nearby remained conveniently motionless so Max concentrated on the one jammed between his razor teeth. If he could stomach this one he'd pack that other one away too, he thought, as he snapped the dying snake's back one final time and threw the body down to tear it open with his teeth.

And then the rains bowled him over.

His killing frenzy had blinded him to change in the light. For the skies had darkened terribly and then flashed and a vast angry noise beat about his ears. Now, torrents of rainwater battered him down against the ground. Deep puddles opened up all around him and the water boiled in them. The dead snake swirled this way and that, as Max struggled for purchase in this new mudfield sent to drown him.

He managed to keep his feet and struck out, choking on water and mud, towards a section of wall beside the hot grass box still half-visible behind the deluge. But the relentless downpour proved too strong for him and he had to twist back under the failing canopy of the fruit trees and scrabble deeper into the fruit tree field.

ℱ

The storm penetrated everywhere, a thunderous battering of water in driving rods, punctuated by blinding flashes and appalling ear-shattering noise. Above him the fruit tree branches whipped this way and that, dislodging fruit and leaves that joined in the downpour.

Max skidded through the bubbling vegetable carpet towards the centre of the field. He needed to find some rising ground. Some tree with roots jutting proud of the flooding, where he could hold a defensive position until the tempest passed.

This ferocity simply couldn't last. The storm would fight itself to a standstill. Things just had to calm down. Max focussed on the thought as he fought his way through the sodden grass, throwing up a wake of muddy water and squinting hard against the driving rain for some hint of refuge.

A big ginger tomcat scowled back at him. It stood only feet away, half hidden in the dark shapes thrown by the lightning against the gnarled base of an apple tree. A farm cat with well-bitten ears and malevolent, yellow eyes, it stood huge and still with a dead fieldmouse clamped between its jaws.

Max pulled up. Checked the distance to the wall behind him, the wall ahead and the nearest tree. Everything was too far away. He was pinned in the centre in the killing ground. Dead centre.

The tomcat jabbed its head to one side, depositing the dead mouse in a safe dry spot on top of a tree root. He gave his massive right shoulder a cursory grooming lick and then stared implacably at Max.

"Well, well, well." He had a deep, mocking voice. "Playtime."

"You're not in the Pig Killers' burrow now," replied Max coolly. "You're out in the wild. See?"

"I've killed hundreds. Out in the wild. Why should you be any different?" smirked the tomcat, looking disinterestedly over his left shoulder. It was a pose designed to show he had such devastatingly fast reflexes that he could take everything at his own languid pace.

"It might work with mice," said Max, "but it won't work with me."

"I've taken your kind," he yawned, "easily."

"Babies probably." Max allowed himself a dismissive shrug.

"You've got the smell of the burrow all over you. The smell of the meat the humans throw to you."

The rain beat down between them. The tomcat had a better sighting, and a drier starting position. But he also had a steady supply of food in the Pig Killers' burrow and Max was used to fighting for his life.

"I eat what I like. I leave what I like." The tomcat looked down at the dead fieldmouse. "I kill what I like."

"You're a big cat but you're in bad shape. With me it's a full time job." Max was quiet but firm. "Now behave yourself."

The tomcat leapt up at the affront. His fur bristled, his back arched as he thrust heavy forefeet out to balance himself for the spring. A savage wailing erupted from deep in his chest. His jagged tail lashed evilly.

"I'll shred you. I'll claw your guts. Hundreds I've killed."

Max flung himself up on his back feet and shrieked back in venomous bursts, "You ready to die for this, pussy cat? Right here. Right now. You better be. Because I am, you fat Pig Killer's kitten."

They stayed snarling and spitting at each other. Waiting for some sign of advantage.

"Don't try it with me, ratface. I'll destroy you," the cat howled eerily.

"Come on, pussy!" Max shrieked. "You're dealing with the Blood and Guts Mob now. Not frightened little mice!"

He didn't know the way this would go. The tomcat was strong, experienced and had taken a lot of pain in his time. Certainly not as tame as Max was making out. It would be close. He could possibly go under. But he had no choice and the cat did.

"Ready to die, pussy? Pussy, pussy, pussy!"

The enraged tomcat began to swell intimidatingly. He bounded off to one side but as he landed, he suddenly screamed and then pulled his left forepaw back as if it had been burned. As he was thrown off balance Max darted forward to within a couple of feet, and again reared up into his back foot display.

"Eat and die. That's what we do out here, pussy. Eat and die. I'm ready for either. Every day. You want to die, pussy? You want to die right now?"

Something was really bothering the tomcat. Keeping his mind off the job. He couldn't stay combat ready. Max dropped to all fours, eyes narrowed, snarl at its widest. "Puss off, you fat parasite!"

The cat took two awkward steps back to its fieldmouse. He sneered at Max, "I'm not going to kill you tonight, you black tailed rat. I think I'll kill you tomorrow."

And with that, he snatched up his fieldmouse and loped off towards the fruit tree field edge in the direction of the Pig Killers' burrow. Max noticed he was limping badly. Something had happened to his left forepaw.

Max moved up to where the cat had landed. Scuffed into the ground was the broken, sodden body of Darren the wasp. His wings were crushed into the mud and his thorax flattened into them but his abdomen stuck up into the rain. From it, albeit it battered from the impact of the tomcat's landing, protruded the ruptured remnants of Darren's sting and its venom sac.

Useful at the last, thought Max. And then he looked around to see if the storm showed any signs of blowing itself out. He had to get out of this weather.

Graham thought he was going to shake himself to pieces. His nerves were in tatters. The smell of cat. The smell of stoat. The driving rain. The awful raging storm pressure in his large delicate ears. It was almost too much to bear.

He huddled in a crevice formed as a sprawling tree root had struck momentarily out of the packed earth before binding back firmly beneath the leaf mould. The tree itself was set – just his luck – in the middle of the fruit tree field. All around was empty space. Dangerous empty space.

And no sign of Lisa and Wendy. Or his brother Roger. They'd all scampered away the moment the smell of cat had invaded the fruit tree field. He, utter utter idiot, had his greedy head stuck in a fallen apple, guzzling the sweetest fruit right next to the core and when the reek of death finally intruded upon him, he'd missed his chance of headlong flight.

Graham belched sadly, his fear rendering the fruit pulp virtually indigestible. He felt full and sick and very, very alone.

His quivering nose picked up the return of cat, this time with the aching smell of dead mouse. Not a fieldvole. Not one of his own. But dead and close-by nevertheless. A meal in readiness.

Perhaps the cat would be satisfied. Perhaps it was enough. He rubbed his whiskers briskly, flexed an ear in the damp rain and knew he was fooling himself. With cats it was never, ever enough.

If they weren't hungry, they'd kill anyway. Eventually. Once they'd grown bored with your screams. Or so much of you had come apart in their claws that they didn't know which bit to torment further. He shook the thoughts way. Returned to the comfort of his quivering.

The cat was coming closer and closer. Graham crammed

himself under the root, reducing his body space till it was leaf thin. He shook and he sniffed and he listened.

There was something unusual about the cat's walk. Yes, a strange rhythm. It was almost as if it only had three legs.

It was hurt. Graham's eyes popped with panic. There was nothing crueller or more vindictive than a wounded cat, driven to ease its pain by inflicting it on others. On voles like him, who'd run out of space, time, luck and, if he were honest with himself here, the will to live.

The smell of cat was on him. Inches from the root. The awkward foot falls resounded through the earth. The awful warning of the dead mouse smell filled Graham's nostrils. He waited for his time of pain.

But the cat simply pounded off past him, hissing small angry breaths through its nostrils, angry snorts muffled by what must be the dead mouse in its jaws. It wasn't stopping. It was taking its mouse somewhere else.

Graham was astounded. It couldn't be moving past. He was a vole. He didn't get breaks like this. If there was a cat in his vicinity, it killed him. That was the way of things. But he listened as the footfalls faded past, and the smell of cat grew lighter and lighter on the air.

Then before he could realise quite how terrified he was, he scampered out from under the root and traced its twisting length to its full extremity. The rain drenched fruit tree field extended before him. The grass, where not trampled flat, whipped around in the gusting rain.

It was noisy. It was busy. It didn't have a cat in it. It was time to go.

His little legs pumped without cease. Even when he'd run himself into a sodden tussock, lodging his head firmly into the unyielding tangle of mud and grass, his legs kept churning away in the direction of the wall. The nearest wall. There by the hot grass box.

Lisa and Wendy and Roger had run that way. Perhaps they were waiting for him.

He kept pushing out little squeaks. Squeaks of fear. Squeaks of determination when rivulets of water pushed him away from the wall with their contraflows. Squeaks of exasperation when the muddy ground barred his way, dragging him back to a desperate standstill. Squeaks of terror when he remembered how fast the cat had come back.

He kept his head down for one last effort to make the wall, scrabbling through planes of muddy water now until he found himself clambering across a submerged snake. He bit and fought and scrambled and squeaked his fear out, as the snake coiled clumsily around him until his paws plunged into a bloody gash at the base of its head, and he realised it was dead.

It was a shock to kill or cure, and it launched him, eyes shut and feet scratching and slithering, out of the mudslides and up onto the water slicked stones at the base of the fruit tree field wall.

Graham couldn't quite believe he'd made it there, jammed against the side of the hot grass box, with the rain slashing down on him and trying to wash him off the slippery stones of the wall's base, to drown in the roiling slurry beneath.

A rodent energy possessed him. He wouldn't go down now. Not to cats, rain, snakes or lightning. He was a field vole. He had to hide. And hide he would. The primal urge of escape and evasion gave him new power. A kind of coward's rage that drove him up the slippery stones and into a cleft between them where his sore feet could finally gain some true purchase.

His lungs were at bursting point, his coat drenched, his whiskers torn and bedraggled. But he heard the rain beating down outside the wall now, as he scurried on inwards, and felt a glow of triumph that he had outrun it.

He knew darkness. He knew small corners. He'd curl up in his own element and digest the fruit pulp hanging heavy in his stomach. He hadn't sicked it up and that was a miracle in itself. What had he been thinking of, carrying all that extra weight on his flight from sudden death?

What was a meal, when your life was at stake?

He turned into a large cavity set in the dry heart of the wall, and as he instinctively made for the far corner, he realised that in his relief he'd been ignoring his sense of smell. And his sense of smell had been screaming at him.

He stopped. And listened to it now.

It said stoat. In here with you.

"Come on in," Max's voice eased out of the darkness. "I'm about to have lunch."

ℬ

Fed, rested and dry if a little blood smeared, Max pushed his head out of a fissure high up on the fruit tree field wall on the meadow side.

The sun was shining bright and low in the late afternoon. The sky was innocent and blue and the storm just an unlikely memory. Max widened his eyes to accustom them to the fresh clear light and then blinked at what he saw.

The tall grasses of the meadow were topped by an elaborate intricacy of spiderwebs that spanned the whole field and glistened back at him with crystal intensity.

The web cover was light as air, with highlights as sharp as ice that fired the sun's light back to him and with woven skeins that shimmered, awash with the reflected azure blue of a safe September sky. And above all this, red admirals danced and fluttered as if unsure which part of the brilliance to set down in.

Max could hear the far off sounds of larks calling to each other now the afternoon skies were theirs again. The passing growl of a coughing box back on the Roaring Road. The distant clanging of the humans' pointed burrow over by the duckpond.

Even the pig reek was wafting back in as life returned to

some kind of normal. And with that, Max decided to follow the wall down as far as it went and then take the meadow side of the ditch back to the Roaring Road. That way he should stay out of water and trouble. Although of course nothing was guaranteed.

He took in the shimmering network of webs again. Maybe Waldo was right. Maybe it was a beautiful world. At least for the time being. Then he looked down to find his footholds down the side of the wall and into the long grass and saw he had a torn section of Graham's ear stuck between his fore toes.

He pulled it out and spat it off to one side. And then he started on his way home in the warm sunshine, as some swallows dipped over the meadow, off to find some shiny to perch on and chatter about their plans for moving on.

# October

## An Early Massacre of the Innocents

The Oak Wood was the only place in Max's country clinging steadfastly onto its leaves. It remained a rolling mass of green beyond the lay-by, punctuated by white clumps of dead hemlock stalks that clung with equal defiance to the soil amongst the trees.

The beeches were golden now, though. And conkers and chestnut leaves plummeted like erratic rainfall, along with withering leaves from the birch and the maple, as the season slowly faded all around him. The redwings were back plundering the red berries of the bryony that strangled the hedging plants and the humans' shiny along their boundaries cutting field from field. The year was dying.

Max was making his way up to the humans' green patch. He'd spent the morning skirting the Oak Wood and had killed once, a bank vole foraging in the scrubland linking the Oak Wood to the stream. After that he'd found nothing there but fungi.

He hadn't gone back to the Roaring Road and to the lay-by. There were humans there fiddling around in their coughing boxes. Anything edible would be hidden securely in the oxtongue that thrust bristly yellow flowers across the verge. Instead he'd worked his way back across the hardpacked stubble of the wheatfield towards the duckpond and the humans' green patch.

It was a dangerous time in the skies. Young sparrowhawks had finally been forced from the nest and chased from their parents' territory. They cruised the airways, inexperienced and resentful enough to dive on anything they thought would provide fuel for their journey into a wild, murderous independence. So Max checked the airways every few seconds.

Halfway across the wheatfield, the sound of small explosions floated in on the air from way back in the country beside the Oak Wood. The humans were slaughtering pheasants there, making sharp noises and smoke that caused them to plummet from the sky.

Pheasants. An easy bird, stupid and slow on the ground. He'd tried before to move into their country and pull them down or plunder their eggs. But he'd found an aunt of his and a cousin hanging dead and rotting from a strand of shiny leading into the scrub, tied there by the humans who had scorned to eat them.

The sight and the smell had convinced him there were enough dead stoats in the area, and he'd hurried away before the humans fell on him and organised a grisly family reunion. He never went there now.

Safely over the field, he'd hurried across the lane and into the shelter of some patches of Michaelmas daisies, at the far end of the humans' green patch where it faded into the Hazel Coppice.

Between the green patch and the Hazel Coppice a ditch meandered its way through to the human burrows clustered together up towards the big pointed burrow with its field of tall stones. Around the burrows were the humans' flower-fields and other small green patches. These humans didn't keep pigs like the Pig Killers, but he'd heard they kept rabbits instead. Someone else had heard Derwent the kestrel calling to his surviving young something about chickens up there. Nobody was sure though.

It was cold enough and things were tough enough for him to try and find out. Chickens matched pheasants in their stupidity and their eggs were bigger. What's more, the humans never made explosions around their burrows and no stoats were hung up to die outside them. That and the hunger had convinced Max it was a risk worth taking.

The ditch often ran with brackish water but now it was filled with dead leaves in varying shades of gold, russet and brown and with Dogwood leaves strewn like purple smoke amongst them. Max nosed his way under and ran along, staying just above the icy wet mud at the bottom but keeping safely hidden beneath the rotting leaf canopy.

Of course he wasn't alone. Slugs and snails had inched their way down from the hazel suckers to forage amongst the mulch, and ground beetles powered their way through the leaf mass in search of ants and springtails. Max snapped up anything that directly crossed his path, but he couldn't let it interfere with the main business of the day. The rabbits and the chickens and the chickens' eggs were his focus now and he needed to maintain momentum both physically and mentally. If he was going to move into exposed human territory, he had to leave his fear far behind.

He was accustomed to the resistance from the leaves now and was moving at speed. The ditch ended up alongside the outer wall of the first of the human burrows and he prepared himself for the next stage in the infiltration. First he had to make a risky examination of the wall base to find an entry point. Then he had to slip through and gain a better idea of the territory. After that, the risks didn't bear thinking about.

So he thought of rabbits and chickens and chickens' eggs and increased his pace through the rustling leaves and then somebody jumped across his path. The collision was too quick for defence or attack and an involuntary loss of control was jolted through him.

All progress stopped. Max fell to one side; half exposed in the top of the ditch, he shook his head to collect his wits. Then the rage welled in him and he scrabbled back on all fours, twisting around in the leaf mass, chattering and snarling. But there was nothing coming at him.

"Yes," concluded a deep voice wryly. "What the world needs now is another stoat in a blinding hurry."

"Ted?" Max stood on his back legs and searched around for the toad in the leaves.

Ted's head appeared in the leaf surface beside him and at that moment both creatures realised they were in daylight. They shrunk back under simultaneously and found themselves aligned in the mulch and the leaf mass.

"Why do you have to play the diseased rabbit in my ditch?" Ted sounded more weary than petulant. "We like it quiet in here."

"We? Who's we?"

"Me, the slugs, the snails. My last supper."

"Ted. You're in the main run into the humans' burrows."

"And I'll be only too glad to be out of it." Ted sighed deeply.

"Miserable I can deal with. But miserable and talking a load of Heron's droppings...." Max turned to move on but a stoat's curiosity got the better of him. "Where exactly are you going?"

"I'm going to sleep, Max. Because I have had this year right up to here." The toad blinked sad, bulging eyes. "I came in here to pack away a few slugs for the journey. Something to tide me over and, bang, all of a sudden I'm nutted by some Blood and Guts merchant racing through my bedtime supper."

"Not that time again, is it?" Max turned back to his route and his plan. "Oh well, see you in the warm. If we make it."

"Where you off now?" Ted was suddenly agitated.

"Up the burrows. Rabbit raid. Chicken, if I get lucky." Then, resenting giving a toad his plans for survival, "What's it got to do with you?"

"That's where I sleep, up there." Ted was aghast. "A little burrow all made of look-through. Back of one of the flower-fields. Six big sleeps I've had there."

"And?"

"You go in and stir them all up, killing their rabbits and what not.... Well, I'll never make it in, will I?" Ted sighted fresh horrors in his imagination. "Humans will be running around everywhere. Shouting. And squishing things."

The toad couldn't believe his annual programme was going to be torn apart. After six years running, he just wasn't equipped for a change of plan this late in the day. Max could almost smell his melancholy.

"I just want to get out of the way, Max," said Ted, sadly. A huge sigh shook him and rippled the leaf mould around him.

"You know the territory up there then? After all these sleeps?" Max prodded through Ted's despair. "You know the ground, right?"

"Just up to the look-through burrow in the flower-field. I never go further than that."

"Is it near the rabbits?" Max kept his voice low and as measured as he could. He still hadn't made up his mind which move he was going to make and Ted's sleep depended on it.

The toad's eyes bulged at the realisation. "No!" he cried. "It's in the first flower-field. The rabbits and the chickens sound like they're way down the ivy wall! In some of the burrows nearer the field of tall stones."

"Then I better move on past it, hadn't I?" prompted Max. "I mean I'm only interested in rabbits and chickens, aren't I?"

The toad let drop a tear of relief, which ran into the mulch between them, "Oh yes, that's all you're after, isn't it!" he concluded joyously. And then, "I appreciate this, Max."

Max stood up and chattered around to dispel all the introspection, then he dropped onto all fours and pushed his head very close to the toad's. "I'd get a move on, Ted, if I were you. I can't hold back on my schedule."

The toad watched a particularly fulsome slug emerge beside him. "I'll make this the last one, then," he offered.

Max nodded, "I'm going in now. And if it gets interesting up there, you'll want to be well tucked away, won't you?"

Ted made appreciative noises. But his mouth was full of slug. Max submerged under the leaf canopy and then built his pace up again towards the ivy wall and all the mayhem it would enclose.

"You moving, Ted?" He called back. Then he wiped the toad from his mind. He was too close to humans now to let his attention wander from the job at hand.

The ditch curved gently round to run alongside the first human burrow. It was scarcely a ditch at all now and eventually he stopped and pulled his head free from the leaves to survey the human burrow's outer wall.

It was built of red squared off stones and a small door of black wood was set in it a few feet further on. Max prised his head under it but all he could make out were shrubs and flowers, and the pervasive smell of humans. Not a sniff of rabbit or chicken. Not a glimmer of Ted's look-through winter shelter either. Maybe they'd broken it up. The country was strewn with broken look-through. Humans broke a lot of it.

Max pulled his head back and then followed the base of the wall further round to where it joined another. This was an older wall with crumbly stones held in place by ancient ivy and this ivy gave Max some small hiding place as he raced along testing the air for the smell of food.

The ivy had thrown out late yellow flowers filled with nectar and these had gathered a tired community of hoverflies. Dickering around amongst the stragglers on the lowest blooms was Waldo the wasp. As Max's head passed a few inches beneath him, he called down hoarsely, "Oi, Stoat! Where's your manners?"

Max stopped and looked up sharply. "Hello, Waldo. Didn't spot you there amongst the flies."

"Hoverflies," sneered Waldo. "Not a decent sting between them."

Spattered with pale nectar, the wasp maintained an unsteady grip on his ivy flower. His wings still whirred heartbeat fast as he adjusted position, but somehow the dynamism was gone.

"Finished with the apples, then?" asked Max.

"Apples are gone, picnics are gone, most of the flowers, nearly all the fruitflies. Can't fathom it. World's petering out." Waldo crawled back into the flower, realised he'd emptied it and shuffled back out again.

"Know anything about any rabbits?" asked Max.

"Further round," snapped Waldo. "All packed away in case they catch cold. Can't even get to their dinner." He revved his wings and then stopped. "World is petering out, isn't it?"

"Not a lot of wasps about, certainly." Max scanned the ivy, "Just you, I'd say."

"One minute you're hatched. Then you're a wasp. Then one day you're not a wasp." Waldo wobbled on his petal. "Where's the sense in that, Max?"

"I never look for the sense, Waldo. Can't eat it, can you?" Max stood down. "Any chickens up there?"

"After the rabbits, there's a rhododendron climbs right over the wall and back of that there's a chicken burrow." Waldo sounded wistful. "Used to be a good few scraps there."

"Why aren't you up there after them, then?"

"I'm alright here, Max." Waldo paused, tired and a little defeated. Then he rallied. "Knock out an egg for me, eh?"

Max tucked in under the ivy cover. "See you around, Waldo."

The wasp watched the stoat's barely perceptible movements in the foliage until he disappeared from view. "I don't think so, Max. I don't think so," he said quietly to himself.

A large hoverfly loomed into the mouth of his flower and Waldo sent an angry warning out with his wingbeats. But he was just going through the motions as the day petered out around him.

As Max powered along beside the old wall, a warm, earthy reek came to him, subtly at first and then with ever increasing intensity. Rabbits!

Packed away from the cold or not, they were somewhere behind the wall and wherever they were, there had to be a way in. Yet, if Waldo was so sure they'd been tidied away securely, there might not be a way out. He'd eat alright, but he could end up trapped amongst the rabbits while vengeful humans fell upon him. He didn't relish dying on a full stomach.

Instead he'd push on and scout for chickens. If he got into their roosting area he might pull an egg away or snatch a dozing hen. It all sounded far less risky than breaking into a sealed rabbit burrow. Anyway, once he'd had sight of the Chicken Situation, he'd be in a position to make a proper decision.

The rhododendron overshot the wall, as Waldo had said. But the wasp hadn't mentioned the jagged buttress holding the wall against the strain, and the fissures running at its base. Of course the wasp flew everywhere, he wouldn't be looking for access points but Max took full advantage. He rummaged in the crumbling pointing and then slipped into the heart of the ancient wall. A couple of twists and turns and he was through to the human flower-field, safely hidden under the bulk of the massive plant.

From the rhododendron's fringe he made a long slow scan of the killing ground. On one side, grass ran away towards a jumbled human's burrow made from dark red stones almost as old as the wall. On the other, were green patches and random clumps of flowers and shrubs and off in a far corner stood a patchy wooden burrow, surrounded by a fence of very old shiny. The shiny was browned by the rain and the years. And between this old shiny and the little shabby burrow, walked chickens.

Chickens calmly taking the air. Chickens without a care in the world. He'd made it. He was through to the land of plenty.

Max sprinted for the nearest shrub on the way down to the chicken burrow, checking the other burrow for humans. The only sign of life was a wagtail dancing along the crest of it. It stopped for a moment as it caught sight of Max speeding across the green patch.

"Judy!" Adrian the wagtail sung out. "There's a stoat in here. Watch out."

Judy, his mate, preened herself at the tube of warm stones that rose from the centre of the burrow's roof. "Don't be silly, Adrian. It can't get up here now, can it?"

"Can't it?" Adrian was unsure. His only child had changed from a wagtail to a huge cuckoo-like thing for no apparent reason and then had suddenly disappeared. After that, Adrian wasn't very sure about anything.

"And if it does get up here, we can fly away, can't we?" Judy had seemed unperturbed about their child's disappearance. Once the nest was empty she'd just gone back to feeding herself. And preening.

Adrian thought this over. "Yes we can, Judy," he agreed. But by then the stoat had disappeared too, so the problem didn't arise any more. "I think I'll have a bit of a sing."

"You do that, dear," Judy encouraged him absently. "You could do with a nice sing, couldn't you?"

So Adrian started a bubbling little song while Max crept on his belly into a small clump of shrubbery just a few feet from the chickens' old shiny. He stopped, listened and looked and tried to assess whether the terrain and the conditions called for a headlong shock assault or a sideswiping hit and run raid.

As Max debated the mechanics of their slaughter, the chickens carried on a desultory non-conversation, filling the gaps in an otherwise mind-numbing social stasis. A kind of paralysis seemed to affect them all. There was no new food to rush for. The new young rooster had been shut away for causing social discord and the stamping of careless feet on half-forgotten eggs. So they called to each other listlessly, to reaffirm they'd missed nothing and indeed there was going to be nothing to miss.

"What?"

"What?"

"Eh?"

"What? What? What?"

"Ohh."

"What?"

It was cyclic, comforting, and drowsy. And in its somnolent rhythm Max slunk up to the old shiny and pushed his nose between the scuffed earth and the tired bottom strands. These birds were asleep on their feet. They wouldn't even wake up when he bit into them.

He wriggled his shoulders in after his head, sizing up a black hen staring into the middle distance no more than three feet away. He'd take it down, drag it under the chicken burrow and devour it. Then he'd lie low until the next one wandered into range. It really was too easy.

The dog hit the shiny at full speed, catapulting itself back onto the grass and springing Max away with it. It was an adult Labrador and it was beside itself with fury, bellowing and scrabbling. Happily for Max, this slathering outrage had robbed it of the close quarter control and co-ordination it needed to make sure of the kill.

Still, it had only lost the initiative momentarily and with its size and power back under control, its finishing would be deadly. Max rolled onto his back as the dog scrambled round to stand over him and slashed with his teeth at the unprotected underbelly. If he could manage to stay underneath the animal, he might unsettle it. He looked for the soft target, the screaming parts, and found it was a bitch. More bad luck.

"Mabs!" a human female screamed out.

"She's got something, Mum!" screamed another.

The humans were running down to help the dog finish him and this gave the brute new impetus. She jabbed her head left and right, dancing in an erratic circle and trying to flush out the half-sighted razor toothed intruder into less vulnerable ground. "Come out! Come out!" she yelled, but her breathing was showing signs of fear. And her footwork felt less assured.

"Mabs! Leave it!"

Max stuck as close to Mabs' belly and dugs as he could manage. Her paws pounded down on him, raking him with her heavy claws but he kept circling with her looking for an exit point. Then suddenly, as she whirled back on herself to wrongfoot him, he sprung through her back legs and made for the evergreen bushes flanking the wall behind the chicken burrow.

"Mabs!"

"Is it a rat?"

"She's not like this with rats."

The dog bounded after him, raging at him, followed closely by the human females shrieking to her and to each other.

"Fox? Is it a fox?"

"Just shuttup and bring her back, Sally."

"Mum! I only said."

"She could get hurt! Sally! For Christ's sake! Mabs!"

Max hit the wall so hard he climbed two feet up it before turning and scurrying behind the thicker branches of the old climber, towards the darkness and the impenetrability of tight, small places. The dog hit the wall seconds behind him and jammed her head between the crumbling masonry and the arterial branches, winded and choking on her own spittle.

"Mabs!" shrieked the youngest female. And a human hand grabbed the dog by the collar and hauled her out into the light.

"Good girl," said the older female, who could hardly speak for breathing so heavily.

Max stayed crushed into the root bowels of the ancient climber. He couldn't get out but the dog couldn't get in. Slowly he brought his heart and his lungs back under control and checked the scratches down his flanks were just superficial. Then he listened keenly for sounds of further pursuit.

"Mabsy, Mabsy, baby," cooed the younger female, "did it hurt you, baby?"

"She's fine. Must have been a bigger rat than she's used to," panted the older one. "Let's take her back inside. I'll get your father down with the gun, when he gets back."

He heard all three of them walk heavily away. Mabs growling threats back to him. Threats they both knew she couldn't make good unless she got him in the open. And he wasn't going to let that happen now.

Max curled up amongst the roots, feeling the shock seep into his body. He could afford to wait and let it clear his system. Let his muscles stiffen and then relax, before he made fighting use of them again. It would be dark soon and the chickens would still be there. He was better than a dog in the dark. He knew that. And if his luck held, he knew he was a lot better in the dark than a trapped chicken.

On the burrow roof, Adrian started his wagtail song again. It sounded implausibly cheerful and Max ignored it, to sink into a healing sleep.

֍

"Oi! Frank! Beak off!"

"Beak off, yourself! This is my ground."

The shrill, chinking cries cut across the dusk, penetrating the shadows and intruded on the stoat's waking dreams.

"You're a tired, old bird, Frank! Going to take you out one night."

"Big tough blackbird, eh? Flapping wren more like."

Max peered out of the creeper. The humans and the dog were long gone. He listened to Frank and the other male blackbirds exchanging their traditional dusk challenges. The sparrows would be off and running soon.

"Here we are! All together!"

"All together! Ever so nice!"

There you go. Stan and Jean, his wife, and Morris, her brother, along with a sizeable array of cousins and second cousins, aunts and uncles all roosted in the hedgerow trilling out a message of mutual support and community spirit. Defiantly cheerful as the day faded coolly away.

"Ever so nice! All together!"

"And far too many to try to eat!"

The light was going fast and with the darkness came the frost. Max stretched his muscles, easing out the last of the shock and the stiffness from the chill evening. He'd take a run round the perimeter before making his approach. He had to be loose and light on his feet, both to make the kill and to get away with it.

It would do no harm to ensure the dog was shut up in the burrow and the humans were hiding away for the night too. If the dog heard something and brought the humans out, Max would need all the time he could get to make it through the ivy wall and back into the safe confusion of the Hazel Coppice.

So he ran the length of the back wall across to the human's burrow, picking up a few quiet chicken noises from their burrow as he passed. Night had fallen now but bright yellow lights shone through the look-throughs in the walls of the burrow until shadowy human forms dragged noisy covers across them and plunged the flower-field back into frosty moonlight. Max listened to the humans moving about inside, calling to each other. Then the incessant babbling noise they often had in their coughing boxes started, so it sounded as if they're were many more of them in there than there really was.

They were making their noises. They weren't paying him any attention. And they had deluged themselves with yellow light so that if they came outside the moonlight would smother them. They would be slow and awkward, like blind baby mice feeling their way from the litter, although probably not quite as tasty.

These were as favourable as conditions ever could be with humans. So, it was time for the kill. He turned and moved quietly back towards the chicken burrow.

He stole in under the dirty old shiny, sunk to the ground and kept very still. If there was going to be any squawking alarm he wanted it now while he could still slip away easily. But all was still. Then he noticed a wooden slat in a corner that was old and worn. He moved across and the damp wood crumbled away as he thrust his bullet head between it and the frosted earth.

"Oooh?" a chicken murmured inside.

"What?"

Max froze. But the conversation was short-lived. Too short perhaps to draw the dog's attention back up at the human burrow. Or perhaps the babbling noises had claimed its attention instead.

He tiptoed inside the burrow. Into its soft straw, spattered with droppings and into its warm, almost yeasty smell and the regular breathing of a dozen, cosy, sleepy bodies.

He lay close to the ground, opened his eyes wide and waited for his vision to adjust. Slowly two ranks of chicken beds appeared to him, one above the other stretching away on either side of the burrow. The beds were filled with dry straw and the dry straw was compressed by healthy, brooding chickens. None of whom seemed to have noticed that death had slipped in among them.

One chicken alone would keep him going for a day. And if he could drag away two, and a few eggs. Well. He could feel the appetite, the desire, and the sense, above all, of plenty beginning to overwhelm him.

A wave of elation coursed along his spine. He had breached the human's chicken burrow. Days of eating were ranged before him. Healthy adult birds with no hope of escape. Resting on top of large, fresh, full eggs, no doubt about it. The fruits of days and nights of danger and anxiety had simply been placed here at his disposal. Opportunities like this just didn't happen.

He should have made a plan. Picked out the victims, settled the order of taking them and the place to drag them out through. But this unheard of abundance triggered a deep, unfettered joy. He rose up on his hind legs as a primal delirium surged through him and chattered out his delight and his driving lust for their blood and flesh.

At once the nearest hens started to squawk and flap.

"What? What?"

"What! Ooh! Oooh!"

He hurriedly bit through the neck of the loudest, pulling her thrashing body out of her bed as her blood pumped over him. Immediately another hen thrust her neck into his killing zone and he scrambled over the first bird to pull her down.

The tiny burrow filled with feathers and scuffed up straw and dust and hysterical chickens. Max leapt along the top row of the beds on one side, slashing down at the birds as they offered up their necks.

They really shouldn't be doing this, he thought as another one ran towards him screaming at him to take her. He only needed one or two. Mice might panic and voles might freeze but he had never come across a creature that jostled and squawked like this to be despatched.

He was encumbered by dying, thrashing birds. He was blinded by their blood and feathers. But the survivors just wouldn't behave like they wanted to survive. They wouldn't run away and they wouldn't calm down. They simply ran at him and demanded he comply with their death wish. The kill rate was draining him and he tore at the plump breast of a bird dying wedged between the lower and upper tiers, tearing away the bloody flesh to fuel the slaughter.

The meat was good, but the feeding was frenzied. There was no satisfaction, no sense of hunger being sated in any normal way. He killed. He devoured. He killed again. He tore at the feathers and flesh pressed upon him. He smashed eggs and sucked out yolks and embryos alike, as the pandemonium rose about him, swamping the normal protocols of predator and victim.

Then through the mayhem, he heard frenzied barking as the dog advanced and a hoarse cry as a male human ran with it.

"Get a light and the other gun." The male was out of breath.

"Someone must have left it unlocked!"

"Oh no, Geoff," the female's anger capped her anxiety, "don't try to dump that on me!"

"Well a bloody fox got in there somehow!"

Max backed into the far corner of the burrow and slunk to the ground. He merged immediately with his surroundings. After all, he was covered in feathers and straw and blood and all around him were dead and dying chickens. He gulped down the last of the liver he had managed to rip from the black hen that lay across him. The adrenaline and the fresh meat pounded through him and he bared his fangs as the door to the burrow was jerked open and the human male thrust his head in.

He held a bright light in one hand and one of their exploding sticks in another. There was a smell of sweat, oil and old explosions in the air. "Keep the dog out!" he yelled over his shoulder and then played the light over the carnage inside the burrow. "Jesus! Jesus Christ!" his yell broke into a sob and then he gathered himself. "Sally?"

"Yes Dad?"

"Don't come anywhere near. Take Mabs back up the house."

"Why?"

"Just do it, love. Please."

The elder female joined the male at the door. She seemed worried by the male's change of voice "What is it. Geoff?" The light played out over the blood and feathers again. Max shrunk down into the gore as the female wailed "Oh no! Oh, my God!"

"Bastards. Murdering bastards." The male was broken voiced.

"Killed the lot. For spite."

He pulled away, "Sally, let the dog go. She'll find 'em"

The female turned back sobbing and called after him, "Be careful, Geoff. We don't want her hurt too."

"Go on, girl! Go on. Find 'em!" Max heard the man shouting to the dog from farther away. But almost at once the big female was barged aside from the door by Mabs who leapt through barking and snarling at Max in his corner. Max shrank further beneath the dead bird and scrabbled uselessly at the earth behind him.

"I'll kill you. Kill you!" Mabs screamed at him but Max would not reply. The dog knew he was in there. But she didn't know precisely where yet.

"Mabs!" yelled the female. "She's gone mad!"

"Get her out of there!" The big male arrived back and then leant in and tugged at the dog's collar. "I'll take her down the back end, start her there. You see what we can save here."

The bright light disappeared and in the darkness, Max collected his breath and his wits. He could hear dog and man moving away towards the ivy wall and Hazel Coppice, cutting off his escape. So he'd have to find another way. Follow the wall by the creeper he'd slept in and try to find a way into the next flower-field. That would at least put a human's wall between them.

He moved cautiously towards the open door and then turned to look at all the food sprawled out around him. Perhaps he should pull a bird over to the creeper and collect it later. It was tempting. He nosed at a plump hen beside the doorway when he was bathed in silver light. The big female human was back, standing over him with a bright light in one hand and a big black shiny holding thing in the other. The holding things they often dropped by the rotting food box in the lay-by. Behind her was the smaller female carrying a black shiny holding thing too.

Well, they weren't going to trap him in one of those. Max snarled up at the big female at precisely the moment she looked down to her feet and saw him. Max froze under her deafening scream. If she hadn't hurled herself back into Sally she could have stamped him right into the ground. But she did jump back and Sally screamed and they both screamed and Max tore between them through the gate in the shiny and back over towards the creeper he knew.

"Geoff! It's a stoat. Over here!"

"A stoat! Just one?"

Max kept tight against the wall, leaving a trail of bloodstained feathers as he fled away towards the next flower-field. He could hear the dog charging up and down, shrieking with fury. He could hear the females crying and yelling to each other and he could hear the shouts of the male trying to calm them all.

"Listen!" he kept shouting. "Just shut up and listen."

"Just don't shoot that thing near us!"

Mabs tore round and round the flower-field. Picking up Max's old scents and pathways. But Max was drenched with chicken offal. His current smell was altogether different. He ran into the far wall, still under a protective cloak of shrubbery and darted back and forth with increasing desperation, seeking an opening.

Finally, Max found a patch of earth drier and less frosty than the rest. It was packed around a stone set in the base of the wall, with rows of holes set in it. A slight but continuous breeze blew through the holes and this in turn had dried the earth nearby and driven back the frost.

Mabs stopped still in the middle of the green patch and pointed her nose to the sky and scented intensely. Max's bloody reek had been picked up by the wind in the wall and wafted gently just outside the shrubbery that concealed the stone with the holes. Silent for once, Mabs flung herself towards the reek.

"She's got him!" cried the male in triumph.

Max crushed himself into one of the holes in the stone and pushed frantically with his back legs. He could feel the tube of stone engulf him, compressing his bones, closing his lungs, leaving only his tormented rear legs to move. There was a juddering all around him as Mabs hit the wall and tore at his escape route with her claws. The impact jolted his forelegs free from under his ribcage so that he could now

gain purchase with all four feet. His lungs emptied of air but he scrabbled and clawed until his head fired out at the other side of the wall.

He prised himself out onto the earth and gulped in the frosty night air. Pure fear had compressed him and a substantial chicken dinner through an aperture half his width. His digestion wasn't the only thing taking a battering that night.

He slunk under a nearby climber and peered out on the new terrain. Unlike normal fields, flower-fields differed wildly in plants, layout and threats. Max was proud of his chicken raid; he didn't want that triumph to be a short-lived one. So he scanned the night-time flower-field carefully and slowly.

It too had a human burrow at the far end, and a small wooden furrow halfway down with look-through sides. And beside this burrow was a rotting grass box like the Pig Killers' had. And by this rotting grass box, Don the badger was doing something shifty.

Max looked around for somewhere to hole up. Don's bad temper was legendary. And this was the badger-mating season. So Don spent most of his time hunting down young male badgers so he could tear them to pieces and then cornering young female badgers to whom he behaved with equal ferocity.

He was death on legs. And right now he was at his most lethal and intolerant. Max hoped the Labrador from the next burrow would run into him, but knew it was hardly likely. It was something he would have liked to see though.

The noise from the Chicken Keepers and their dog had receded, but Don had turned instinctively the moment Max had penetrated the wall. He'd sniffed at the night with a scowl, and decided there was nothing coming that he could disembowel so he returned to the matter in hand.

The matter in hand as far as Max could see was hidden deep in the rotting grass box. The big badger leant in and scrabbled about with his razor fore claws until finally he gave a hacking cough of triumph and pulled something from the warm mulch.

The moon on the prickles gave them a frosted appearance and Max knew at once that Don had found Cliff the hedgehog's winter sleeping place. Cliff, himself the proud possessor of a vile temper, seemed to be unaware of his early wake-up call, or he may just have been playing his natural defensive game.

Staying curled into a hostile spiny ball will work with most creatures. But as any hedgehog will tell you, a badger doesn't play by any other creatures' rules. That's why you never find hedgehogs in badger country. They flee or they die. Cliff had kept well out of Don's country all year. So Don had come to him. And tonight the badger had become the hedgehog's worst nightmare.

Max could hear the tiny, fear-stricken whimper that belied Cliff's sleeping posture as Don took a firm grip of each end and unrolled him lengthways. Although his underbelly was now undefended against the badger's murderous teeth, Cliff kept his eyes shut and acted dead to the world. Unfortunately the tremors that shook his frame and the squirting droppings that trickled through Don's claws and onto the rotting grass marred his performance.

Don gave an indulgent chuckle and then, almost tenderly, he placed his foul smelling mouth by the hedgehog's ear. "Wakey Wakey!" he roared.

Cliff squealed in terror and his eyes shot open. Just in time to watch Don bite viciously into his stomach. With his teeth sunk into Cliff's writhing body the badger gave a sickening sideways bite and wrenched out Cliff's gutsack. The young hedgehog's scream froze on the night air, and as the blood exploded around Don's jaws, Cliff was already dead.

Don chewed contentedly on Cliff for a while. Then turning to Max's hiding place, he called over between mouthfuls of hedgehog. "Was that you at the chickens, Max?"

Max thought about sitting it out. But he knew that Don would flush him out if he didn't show sufficient respect for his lethal capabilities. "I had a little visit," he acknowledged.

"Naughty boy." Don's eyes twinkled over the gory mess he was making of the hedgehog, and then they suddenly flashed cold.

"You'll give us all a bad name."

Don didn't want disturbances on his foraging patch.

"Won't happen again, Don." The badger raked him with a look. "They're all dead, see."

Somehow this appeased the old bloodletter, "Wasn't you, it'd be them shabby foxes," he grumped, and then peered disgusted at what he'd left of Cliff. "Want the end of this hedgehog?"

"Thanks all the same. I'm off home." And Max carefully followed the wall away from Don and over towards the Hazel Coppice side of the flower-field. "Good night."

Don threw the mangled skin back into the rotting grass box.

"'Spect Brian and Ray'll clear this up tomorrow."

"More than likely."

The badger sniffed around the door of the wooden burrow with the look-through sides, "Ted has his kip in one of these, doesn't he?"

Max kept on moving, "I don't know, Don. He never says." It was the least he could do.

Don was nosing at the rickety door, "I'll give it the once over." He threw an evil glance over his shoulder to Max, "Just for the hell of it."

Max cast his mind back to the slaughter in the chicken burrow, the killing without eating, without necessity, the killing just because there was killing to be done. Maybe that's what separated Don and him from other creatures. Not that they killed to eat. But that killing was their nature. They ate to kill.

He didn't like the thought of being so close to Don. As he picked his way through the ivy wall and back into the Hazel Coppice, he just hoped Ted had found a different look-through burrow for his big sleep.

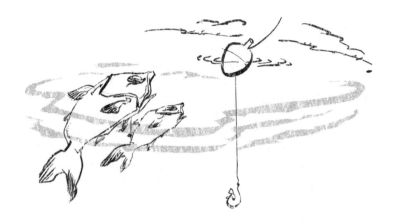

# November

## The Kindness of Strangers

The world was filled with fallen leaves, a riot of colour at ground level becoming progressively more sodden and obstructive. It was cold and damp. The skies an unrelenting grey. And just moving around seemed to exhaust many of the lay-by regulars.

On a track beside the lane down from the Pig Killers' fruit tree field to the lay-by, Max had found the bodies of two adult shrews, worn out by the simple necessity of continual hunting. Tiny though they were, they lived with a three hour deadline of starvation. Every day meant a desperate calculation of energy out and fuel in. Hunting and killing, when an unsuccessful hunt would kill you, made for a critical path extreme even by the standards of the Blood and Guts gang. The pressure made shrews vicious, desperate creatures and had finally told on these two. Max cleaned them up without ceremony. To his mind the world was well rid of the combative little brutes.

The coughing boxes seemed especially noisy these days, with more smoke than usual flooding from them. None stopped at the lay-by. But Max had noticed that damp and cold kept them away in numbers. Perhaps the lay-by smelt differently to them in these conditions.

When he finally crossed the Roaring Road the lay-by was empty, except for Frank the blackbird, perched on the rim of the rotting food box. And Frank was not happy. His hearing picked up Max as soon as he broke cover from the hawthorn bush and he turned and fixed him with a brittle expression and an angry warning signal. But once he took in Max's familiar sleek form and the effortless lope, his shoulders dropped and the aggression faded.

"Alright, Max?" It was a listless welcome.

"That's better." Max registered a friendly disapproval at Frank's initially hostile moves. "What's got up your beak this morning?"

"It's cold, damp and the country's full of greedy, flapping blackbirds!" Frank let loose a copious dropping into the rotting food box to emphasise his disgust.

"You don't usually take against your own." Max slipped into the burdock patch to enjoy his friend's discomfort in safety. He remembered the shrews. They spent more time at each other's throat than anything else. It probably kept their numbers down. "What's the problem with blackbirds?"

"There's blackbirds and blackbirds." Frank edged quickly round the rotting food box rim so he could look down on Max to make the point.

"Glad that's cleared up, Frank." Max gave himself over to grooming for shreds of dead shrew.

"There's blackbirds from round here. Local blackbirds who know the rules. The territories. Who's with who. If you get my meaning?" Frank tilted his head to give Max a long, pointed look to make sure he did. "Then there's blackbirds from overseas and the rest. Foreigners. And there's foreigners all over the place."

"It's just that time again," said Max. As a stoat he didn't

suffer any migration problems but it was a big issue with the birds. Come the cold weather a lot flew out to the sun, coming back in the spring to gloat on whoever was surviving. But a lot more flew in from colder climates. And the locals really didn't want them moving in on the limited food stocks.

"Not enough to go round as it is," Frank spouted.

"Not enough what?"

"Food. Space. Females." Frank drew himself up to full outraged height. "One of them was pushing his luck with my Missus."

Frank's wife was of an independent frame of mind. Her call was as loud as Frank's and her temper much worse. She didn't often come down to the lay-by, a fact that seemed to draw Frank to the place.

"What did she make of that, then?" Max enjoyed a good fight story. It passed the time between the real thing.

"Swallowed it down like a fresh, fat worm. All those foreign notes and flutters, you know. Thought she was a chick again. Daft old egg squatter!" Frank shook the memory away with a vicious swipe of his beak. "I had to have a word."

Max sucked air in through his teeth. "Oh dear."

"She'll come back." Frank didn't sound convinced. He slicked down a chest feather and looked gloomily into the rotting food bin. "Bloody foreigners!"

The blackbird took off minutes later. He didn't say goodbye, just flew off in a preoccupied manner towards the Oak Wood. He was either looking for his wife or a fight. And Max reckoned that either way Frank had a fight on his hands. He threw the thought away and returned to the menu. Like a shrew, that topic was never far from the front of his mind.

A forage through the Pig Killers' farm had produced a vole but the farm dog was active again, even if the pigs were depleted in numbers and tucked away in their arcs. The Pig Killers were pulling straw all over the place too. Which all made for hard hunting up there. So he'd made the one kill, fuelled up and come back down to see if the roadside verge was busy.

All he'd found was Frank's migration problems. Still, if the birds were stirred up there'd be hunting opportunities. Neglected nests. Young ones making their way through the crowds of newcomers, vulnerable in the confusion.

He thought of the duckpond; it was a transit point for many. The birds going out used the humans' pointed burrow nearby as a gathering point and the birds coming in used the pond itself as a feeding and refreshment stage. Some of them settled there for weeks.

It would be busy. And where there was busy, there were stragglers.

Max moved across the verge and into the wheatfield, plotting another track towards the duckpond and the green patch. He varied his course automatically in case the hawks had got lazy. It wasn't a sure-fire defensive measure, but he thought it must narrow the odds. And it kept his mind on the job, which in his view was the only way to keep him alive.

He was well across the field when he saw Claire, the female stoat he'd mated with in the spring. She was on her hind legs and a few feet from her an elderly rabbit crouched as if paralysed.

Claire was dancing. A jerky, gymnastic dance which seemed to mesmerise the old rabbit. She threw herself this way and that, dropping occasionally on all fours and moving closely towards her prey. Then she'd be up and dancing again, swaying this way and that.

Max pulled up and watched sadly. The rabbit didn't move. It wouldn't move. It was already dead. It may have died from fear of her, (Some rabbits gave up life when they saw a stoat and it had often made his life easier.), but it looked more likely that this one had been dead for a while. Its eyes had that glazed over, muddy look.

And Claire kept on dancing.

"Claire!" he called over to her, hoping she'd be able to hear him.

She turned at once, although her jerky dance steps continued. As she strained to focus on him he realised his fears had been confirmed. Her once bright and shining eyes were now stricken and tormented. Her grace and balance was now racked by spasms of pain.

The dancing sickness.

"Max!" her voice was brimming with fear and sadness. "Max, it's my head! My head, Max. The pain!"

She shook her head violently to try and dislodge the excruciating pain within. Her eyes bored into his as if, through the fixity of her gaze, she could convey the agonies and the terror she was enduring.

"Oh, Max, the pain! Such pain!"

She danced around in distress, the dead rabbit at her feet forgotten now, if she had ever seen it. And Max stayed where he was, keeping his distance from her. He'd seen others with the dancing sickness. Heads convulsed with pain, feet following the same demented pattern. He'd watched many infected stoats dance themselves into madness.

"I can't escape it, Max! What do I do?" she was frantic.

He hurried on. Nobody knew how you caught the dancing sickness. All he knew was that you didn't survive it. Ever. Agony and exhaustion killed you eventually.

"Max!"

He would rather give himself to a sparrowhawk.

"Max! Where are you?"

She was racked by another spasm, twisting her head back towards the Roaring Road. She steadied herself on her feet, took several deep breaths and then as the convulsions began again she went back into her anguished judder and sway.

Reg and Daphne bobbed up and down on the chill, black water, their briskly paddling feet barely perceptible beneath the pond's surface. On the nearby bank, Daphne's brother Ken stood squat and grumpy in the reeds, picking irritably at some straw embedded in the half-frozen mud.

The wind was slight and chill. From time to time a rook would call bleakly to another but other than that, the birds were not singing.

"I think it's icing up," said Reg, as he scudded round in an aimless small circle. "I can feel it coming."

"We'll have all them foreign geese here in no time," said Ken as he gave a sharp, vicious tug on a mud-spattered stalk.

"Eh?" said Reg, trying to turn back on himself. He found himself beak to beak with Daphne. "Eh?" he asked her.

"Deaf. Or Daft," Daphne commented to whoever would listen.

"Sometimes it's difficult to decide what he is."

Ken waddled down to the waterside, nibbled a wingfeather and continued with his pet hate. "I said Geese, Reg. Slapping around here with their great pink feet. Smashing up all your dinner. Honking in their stupid voices."

"Who?" asked Reg, heading towards Ken now in a rather wavy crescent.

"Deaf and daft. That's what he is," pronounced Daphne loudly, causing two moorhens to get up from their personal clump of reeds and pace jerkily off round the pondside seemingly in search of a little peace and quiet.

"Not just geese either, is it?" Ken threw a beady eye up to heaven. "Couple o' weeks we'll be stuck with a pond crammed full of greedy, fighting, jabbering tourists."

"No peace for the wicked," said Daphne.

"Hundreds of 'em," agreed Reg finally, "shouting and bawling."

"And spitting," added Daphne.

"Lurching." "Snapping." "Stealing." "Bellowing." The three ducks joined their complaints and their voices together in one loud and contented family chorus. "Hissing." "Puking."

"Breaking wind."

"Why don't you shut up?" shouted the male moorhen as he stomped crossly away from them through the pondside overgrowth. But, of course, they didn't hear him.

His mate scrabbled to keep up, calling ahead in tones of increasing desperation, "Alan? Alan! Now where you off to?"

"I've had just about all I can stand from those quacking cretins," snapped Alan, putting his best foot furiously forward.

"They're only making conversation," she protested.

Alan stopped momentarily, and turned his head back to her. "It may be conversation to you, Sheila," he snapped. "It may be conversation to those big-billed idiots. But to me, it is just empty, flapping noise. And I've had enough of it."

"Where we going, though?" she had to dodge to avoid the reeds whipping back at her as he set off again.

"I'm going round to the ramp by the human roost. Get a bit of peace and quiet for a change."

"That's Harry's ramp," warned Sheila, as she tried to tuck in beside him.

"It is not Harry's ramp," retorted Alan hotly.

"He thinks it is. He said so." Sheila was breathless and confused. "Just after he kicked you off it. He did kick you off it, didn't he?"

"I can go there any time I want," said Alan as icily as his anger would allow.

"He pecked you as well, didn't he?" said Sheila earnestly trying to clear things up. "And then he pushed you in the water and said, 'Don't you ever…'."

"Never mind Harry!" Alan's explosive temper echoed

round the pond. "Forget about Harry. I'm going onto that ramp. If Harry doesn't like it, he can flapping well lump it."

"Be careful, Alan," begged Sheila. "Don't lose your temper. You'll only regret it."

Alan stopped again, pecked a twig out of his way, and then turned back to her. "I'm not going to regret nothing. I'm just going to the ramp. But I'll tell you this much. If Harry so much as raises his beak to me, I'm going to really sort him out this time."

"Two grown moorhens like you." scoffed Sheila, nervously.

"You'd think you'd have better...."

"Oh, I don't flapping believe it," said Alan in sudden despair.

"What's happened?"

"There's a pair of humans roosting there." Alan backtracked cautiously into a thick clump of iris and peered round them at the invaders. Sheila looked at him archly.

"Going to sort them out, too, are you?"

Alan backed further into cover, "You're no help to me, Sheila," he said, "no flapping help at all." Then he turned and walked off so fast, Sheila couldn't quite see where he'd gone to.

The two humans were perched on tiny stools at the water's edge, in a clutter of drab canvas bags, waterproof clothes and fishing tackle.

There was a rickety old bench at the top of the ramp, and they'd stowed their lunch on it, in a small confusion of tin foil and thermos flasks. One of them had been up for a rummage through it. He was eating a sandwich as he peered into the still, black water.

"It's far too cold, Mick," he said through a mouthful of cheese and pickle, his breath eventually pluming in the cold morning air.

"They're about," said his friend. "What you got there? Sweetcorn?"

"Cheese and pickle."

"No, what you baiting?"

"Oh, right. Sweetcorn."

"Just a matter of time, Bill, just a matter of time."

A few feet out from the bank, stolidly holding a position about midway between the pond's steely, clean surface and its algae encrusted, overmulched floor, two stout and mature bream stared gloomily at the twin pieces of sweetcorn suspended just in front of them.

"Don't have anything to do with them, Janet," said the larger one gravely. "They're nothing but trouble."

"Brighten the place up a bit, though," sighed Janet. "And let's face it, Rosemary, it could do with it."

"I ate one once." Rosemary stared for a bit longer at the titbit as it swayed in the murk before her. "Shot me straight up through the water-skin."

Janet drifted away a few inches; she'd heard it all before.

"One minute I'm here, eating one of those. And the next thing I know I'm up beyond the water-skin. Swimming on nothing. Choking. With these big, hot things pulling me all over the place, and hurting my mouth."

"And then, all of a sudden, you were back here again." Janet could almost recite it word perfectly. Rosemary's out-of-pond experience came up a good three times a week if not more. Rosemary just forgot she'd told you about it, which was almost as depressing as the murk they were swimming in.

"There's something going on up there, Janet. And it's not natural."

"Get away. It's just where flies come from."

"There's huge things up there just waiting to make horrible noises. And it's all nasty brightness. And it sucks your wet away. "

"Too much air," diagnosed Janet, and then, gently, "You had one of your turns, Rosemary. You know how you imagine things when you have one of your turns."

"You suit yourself," Rosemary swung herself round ponderously, "I know what I know. And I'm not staying round here to be shot up into the bright and hot again."

"Alright, alright." For all the heaviness of her movement, Janet could see her friend was becoming distressed. "Why don't we go down to the warm water tube and eat some brown? You know you like that."

"I wish that pike would eat one of those things," confided Rosemary as the two old friends swam sturdily away. "I wish he'd eat a big one. I wouldn't mind him being shot up there though the water-skin. And never coming back."

Up on the ramp, Mick noticed the wakes on the surface. He drew in his line a fraction, and nodded towards the water movement. "There you go, Bill," he said, satisfied. "Nothing brings them out like a bit of sweetcorn."

"I wish she'd go easy on the pickle," said Mick, scrutinising his sandwich. "It keeps dropping down my sleeve."

From the lower branches of a nearby alder, two pairs of beady brown eyes bored into Bill's back, and then traced the path of crumbs and pickle spills back up the ramp to the rickety bench with its silver parcels, scattered and clumsily half closed.

"Wossee got there, Lenny?" demanded a hoarse, over-energised voice. "Dinner, issit?"

"Corsit's dinner." Lenny's voice was that bit tougher, with the flat tones of the experienced hardcase. "The fat one's only eating it, innee?"

"Gessum, Lenny, I'm starving. Nip darn there and gessum."

"'E's a bit too close for my liking, Martin my son."

"'E's slow, innee?" wheedled a hungry Martin. "They're all slow, innay? Garn, Lenny. Be a doddle for you, this."

"Wot d'ya think I am, suicidal or sunnink?"

"I think yore the hardest squirrel in the patch, Lenny, you know that."

Lenny flared his tail and arched his back. "I am an' all."

"'E's got all sorts of lovely stuff in that silver crinkly." Martin gave a series of excited little hops.

"Wot'm I sposed to do, then? Nick it all?"

"Why not?"

"'E catches me, 'e'll bite my gnawin' head off. That's why not."

All the while the two young grey squirrels had crept down the alder trunk, in fits and starts, until they were just inches from the ground.

"Look, you're almost there now," said Martin.

"Keep your eyes on his mate," said Lenny, suddenly combat ready, and he hopped gingerly onto the killing floor between the safety of the alder and the fishermen's sandwiches.

At that moment, Daphne, Reg and Ken swam round the reed outcrop and into view, a sedate little flotilla that moored only a few feet away from the bobbing fishing floats.

"You want to make the most of this, Reg," said Ken, looking around himself officiously.

"While we can," said Daphne.

"While there's still a bit of space to be had on the water," continued Ken, "what's not full of flapping geese."

"I will," said Reg, suddenly and very loudly. "I will, don't you worry."

"Push off!" shouted Mick, from his stool. And he bent over, picked up a pebble and shied it at the ducks. "Push off out of it."

"Is that bread?" said Ken, eagerly as all three darted towards the splash.

"Can't see," said Daphne, colliding with him. "Mind out."

"Whatever it is, it's sunk," said Reg, bringing his head up from beneath the water and shaking it.

"Wonder if he's got any more," said Daphne and at once all three ducks turned towards the shore and paddled in nearer to the floats.

"Clear off." Bill joined in, clapping his hands.

Lenny had bounded over to the back legs of the rickety wooden bench. Once there he stood absolutely still, and stared down the ramp at the noisy movements of the humans. They seemed completely absorbed in their hostility display to the ducks.

Without a threatening human male in the vicinity, all their aggressive behaviour seemed a bit wasted. Still, if humans wanted to assert their territory against ducks, that was their lookout, and a squirrel's opportunity. He leapt nimbly onto the bench and foraged lightly in the silver crinkly. Within seconds he'd rummaged his way to a result.

"Wot they got?" hissed Martin, who'd now got as far as three small hops away from the base of the tree.

Lenny however, ignored him, and efficiently put away one cheese cracker after another from his newly discovered hoard. One eye on the humans, one eye on what he was demolishing, he maintained enough self discipline not to search for the hidden apple he could smell so close by, until he'd assured himself of a full belly from his first bag of plunder. Lenny was an accomplished marauder.

Martin skipped lightening fast to the back of the bench. He put his forepaws some way up the nearest leg. "Wot is it, Lenny?" he implored. "Nuts? Wheaty stuff? Fruity bits?"

Lenny stopped cramming his face just long enough to say,

"Don't hang about. Get up here while the ducks are keeping them busy." Then he snatched at the crust of a half exposed cheese sandwich and chewed away at that.

Martin was up beside him immediately, grabbing up broken bits of biscuit and packing them away, looking round for the apple he could smell. "They got apple, innay?"

"Get on wiv wot you got," snapped Lenny, his mouth full with bread and bits of celery, "and keep yourself ready for the Big Jump."

If anything, events were getting noisier and noisier at the bottom of the ramp.

"These are stones, Reg." Daphne had made the outraged discovery as she caught one rather neatly in mid air and tried to swallow it. "They're throwing us stones."

"We don't eat stones," Ken told the humans crossly, whilst

trying to dodge the incoming projectiles.

"Get off out of it!" yelled Mick, and then, to Bill, "They'll have all the fish out in the deep if we don't have them away sharpish."

"Stop throwing stuff at them, you daft 'apporth," said Bill. "They'll only think it's food."

"They're not that stupid, surely," replied Mick crossly but nevertheless he sat down and blew on his hands.

Ken, Reg and Daphne milled around in some confusion. Reg tentatively stretched out his neck and tried to nibble what proved to be a very old leaf floating past. "Ugh," he said, "they don't half eat some rubbish these humans."

"That's a leaf, Reg," said Ken, giving up on him.

"Eh?" said Reg.

"Deaf, daft, dozy and dim," said Daphne triumphantly, and she turned round and swam back off the way they'd come. "I'm not hanging round here to eat stones."

"Nor me," said Ken, following suit. "I got better things to do, I have."

Reg hung around for a little while longer. Just in case the humans realised their mistake and threw some proper bread after all. Mick stared at him angrily, going redder and redder in the face. Then, just as he was about to start swearing in earnest, Bill hammered him on the shoulder, and whirled him round.

"Look at our lunch!" he cried. "The squirrels are all over it."

Lenny froze immediately, holding the remnants of his crust. Martin however, had homed in on the apple smell and was trying to dismantle the silver crinkly around it. This seemed to infuriate the humans who started advancing up the ramp. Reg, watching them move off, gave a sharp quack to remind them of who they should really be thinking of feeding.

"Leave that alone!" Mick ran up the ramp towards the bench waving his hands above his head as if signalling to an aircraft.

Lenny dropped his crust and was gone, leaping straight

over the back of the bench and clearing the killing floor back to the alder in three bounds. He hit the trunk more than four feet off the ground, still accelerating, and immediately scrabbled to the reverse side – out of the humans' view. Without pause for breath he launched himself up into the highest branches.

Martin, his forepaws still inside the silver crinkly parcel that smelled so tantalisingly of apple, looked up to find the human upon him. He scrambled frantically along the length of the bench, scattering silver crinkly and biscuit crumbs and knocking a tartan thermos to the ground. Then, as the human towered bellowing above him, he shot out from under the bench's armrest and hurled himself into the dense tangle of a nettle and bramble patch.

Scurrying blindly along the narrow alleys formed by nettle stalks and briar shoots and roofed by thick, impenetrable overgrowth, he became aware of the juicy apple section clamped instinctively between his teeth. And then, deep in the thorny entanglement, safe in the dark from view and human hand, Martin felt a sudden surge of relief and exhilaration. He'd got away with it. He'd taken a human's dinner and lived. Their apple was his alone to enjoy.

He stopped his headlong flight, gathered his breath and looked behind and around him. All he could see was nettle and briar. With a little satisfied smile he hunkered down in the green calm and took the apple section in both forepaws to enjoy it properly.

Max hit him at full velocity smashing his snarling bite into the back of Martin's neck. The blinding impact jarred the apple section from the squirrel's grasp. It flew unheeded down the cramped nettle alley, kicked further on in the dust by the agonised thrashing of the victim's legs.

Gripping Martin's ears and digging savagely ever deeper into his spinal column, Max clamped onto the back of the tumbling, writhing animal until it had jerked out its last desperate lunges for survival.

Mick and Bill heard the grunts and squeals, and saw the

scrabbling disturbing the nettles and the thick brambles.

"What on earth's going on there?" said Mick, quite unsettled.

"They're fighting over our dinner," said Bill. "Vicious things squirrels, you know."

"Right old ding dong, at any rate," mused Mick. "All for a bit of sandwich."

"Well, it's nearly winter. They'll be feeling the pinch."

Max waited for the humans to retreat back to the pondside. He'd waited long enough for Martin, another few minutes wouldn't hurt him.

Crouching in the dark over the dead squirrel he heard the first arrogant, guttural warnings of a formation of Russian geese banking and coming in to land on the pond. He heard the anguished surprise of Reg as he was bowled over and bludgeoned under the surface by the incoming giants. He heard the shouts of fear and exasperation of the fishermen as they watched their lines snagging and their rods jerked into the icy water as the invaders landed and swam to the far shore to survey their new conquered territory.

Then it went quiet. Until, just as Max was settling down to eat he heard one more forlorn cry on the bitter autumnal air.

"Alan? Alan?" cried Sheila despondently as she plodded through the pondweed. "Where you got to now?"

# December

## In the Deep Midwinter

Heather and her sister Audrey were getting more and more worried about Uncle George's behaviour. Whenever they went anywhere near him he'd just turn his back on them and stare away into the middle distance, eyes and nose twitching at the pale, threatening light filtering through the ice curtain which formed a protective barrier between them and the outside world.

Seeping in at ground level, it was the only light here, underneath in the Safe. No light could filter down through the musty, dark mass of the roofness that the humans had so thoughtfully provided so close to the rotting food bin by the Roaring Road.

If you burrowed upwards into the roofness and sniffed in the right darkness, you could detect long gone milk and the dank sweat smell of humans. Heather and Audrey found comfort in that. They could almost convince themselves that nothing would eat through this human smell to get down to them. But Uncle George was having none of it.

Uncle George was too long in the tooth for hope, false or otherwise. "Breed. If we want to survive we must breed," he stammered to himself over and over again, wringing his front paws under his quivering chin. "They can't eat us all. Breed."

"Breed, breed, breed," sighed Audrey, rubbing a frozen ear to reawaken it. "That's all he ever talks about."

"Thank Mouse he's too hungry to do anything more than think about it," replied her sister.

Heather pulled another frozen chunk of roofness down to her. It squeezed and expanded in her grip. It squeezed and expanded as she chewed it. She could feel it squeeze and expand in her tiny, shrivelled stomach. It was hard work living in the Safe.

"Trust in Mouse, Uncle George!" she called over between chews, "Mouse will provide."

"Where's Tony?" replied Uncle George, turning away from her again, flicking his tail in weak petulance. "Tony will know when the Icy White's going. Tony will know where the eating is."

Heather and Audrey exchanged another pained glance; he wasn't getting any easier. Still, seeing that Heather was deeply involved with a large mouthful of roofness that seemed to be prizing her jaws apart, Audrey sighed and went through the litany again.

"Tony drowned, Uncle George. He fell into a look-through stuck in the rotting food box. Remember? And he couldn't get back out and he couldn't drink all the orange water in it, and he drowned. Christine told you all about it," she prompted.

"Christine," Uncle George reflected sadly. "Mouse alone knows what's happened to Christine."

"An owl," snapped Audrey, "right out of the blue. We'd just found some hazelnut shells and – whoosh! – there she was, gone. An owl in broad daylight!" she wondered at it still, then turned crossly back to Uncle George. "I told you about that. I was there."

Heather freed herself from the roofness stuck in her throat. "That stoat got Auntie Bernice and Peter, and probably Lesley." She turned to Audrey, "Well, we only found the ears." Then she scurried over to Uncle George, "June went under the drifting crunchy on the first Icy White day. The rats took Robin and Wendy. Gary swears Gillian and Mary went to the badgers and we haven't seen Barry, Karen and the triplets since we moved over from the thorn ditch and it's too cold and too icy out there for any chance of...."

"Breed. We must breed." Uncle George turned away from the pale light, bunching his paws into his face.

"Perhaps Gary can sort him out when he gets here," said Heather in exasperation.

"You're getting as bad as he is," replied Audrey, pulling down a chunk of squeezy roofness for herself. "What makes you think Gary's going to make it back here either?"

Max hunkered down in the slush and twigs beside the human soft stripy thing and listened to the mice scuffling beneath it. He knew it was pointless to try and get at them. Even if he managed to sneak in under the soft stripy thing on one side, they'd just scurry out of the other three. A pointless waste of energy. He wasn't hungry enough to try that yet.

The icy white had been settling for days. The voles who weren't hibernating were stuck safely away underground with their food stores and the owls were starving from it. One more day of this and tawny bodies would appear in the drifts for the crows to fall upon. Meanwhile other birds were freezing in the air.

There was no let up in the chill and the dampness that slowed reactions, sapped muscle strength and filled the head with a murderous lethargy that only fresh meat could dispel. And there was no fresh meat here.

There was also no way to cross his country to see if things were better up in the Pig Killers' fields or over by the human burrows near the duckpond and the green patch. Any journey of more than a few metres would most likely be his last.

Everything not coated in a protective layer of fat was dying or hidden away in the dryness of underground. For once Max wished he could sleep like a badger. But he couldn't. He could only hunt and kill like a stoat. Or hunt and starve like one.

He stared out into the frozen mist that had settled over everything and flinched as the occasional human slunk past in one of their coughing boxes. With a weak yellow glow in front of each of them, the coughing boxes inched nervously along the Roaring Road like voles on a badger's run.

They'd turned the snow black all around the Roaring Road, crushing the white drifts into shiny, poisonous black chippings that were part ice and part smoke-stained oily. Nothing could survive in all that. Well, nothing you could eat, anyway.

Stan the sparrow fluttered to an untidy halt in a murky, slush puddle inches away from the rotting food box. He cheeped loudly as his feet skidded beneath the frozen mulch, and then, spotting Max beside the human soft stripy thing, he jinked suddenly up to the relative safety of the rim of wire at the top of the box.

Once there he gave a couple of wing jerks, relieved himself into the box interior and then called down cheerfully to the stoat.

"Hello, Max. Murder on the feet, this black icy, isn't it?"

Max stared balefully up at him, out of reach and as infuriatingly chipper as ever. He relaxed from his pre-launch position, trying to keep his belly above the icy.

"Hello, Stan," he murmured. "Haven't seen you around for a while."

"We've been roosting on some nice warm look-through on the top of a human's nest near the pond," said Stan, nibbling at an untidy wing feather. "It's a lovely roost, except that the cat gets bigger every year."

"Big cat, is it?" Max ducked instinctively as another human coughing box loomed up, two weak yellow eyes peering hopelessly out of the pale fog.

"Took two of mine, flapping thing." explained Stan. "We're sleeping on the look-through, when it gets up on the nest cover beside us. I don't think Jean even woke up."

"Nasty," replied Max politely, he could almost taste Jean himself.

"Flapping thing played with Morris for most of the night," continued Stan, "rolling him around the nest-cover. Up and down. Never even ate him."

"What a waste!" Max's stomach felt emptier than ever.

"Do what?" Stan sounded put out.

"What a waste of Morris's life," Max changed tack quickly. He didn't want Stand flying off in a huff. He wanted Stan within striking distance. "Had seasons left in him, didn't he?"

"It was his idea in the first place, poor flapper," Stan wasn't one to brood. "Full of it, he was. 'Stan' he says to me, and I'm going back some time now, Max, 'Stan, we've got to go down to where the humans nest. They leave their food hanging about all over the show.'"

"Well, you can't win them all," replied Max automatically. He could hear a mouse scuffling in safety beneath the soft stripy thing and it irritated him.

"Wouldn't credit it, would you?" Stan hopped along the wire rim of the rotting food box to keep his feet warm. "But they do, you know. They drop lumps of wheaty stuff and nuts and sometimes strips of meat."

"Meat?"

"Not enough to suit you. And no blood at all. Just little strips of salty. Still they come out every day and dump their food down, right where you can have it away – and then they go back in their nests and leave it!"

"How can anyone have that much food?" Max narrowed his eyes angrily at another coughing box as it wheezed past in the fading light. The sickly mist was turning into a treacherous darkness now.

"Well, you can't ignore an opportunity like that, can you?" Stan gave his wings a sad little flutter. "Cat or no cat." And he fell silent.

"So it's just you now, then," said Max.

"Oh, there's some cousins somewhere." Stan fluffed out his chest feathers bravely. "I'll try and catch up with them when the weather breaks. If it ever flapping breaks."

He sat tight, a frozen bundle on top of the rotting food box, lit occasionally by the poisonous yellow vapour thrown out by the coughing boxes as one passed. The darkness joined the cold in crowding in around them.

"There's a chunk of wheaty stuff down here, as it happens." Max spoke carefully up to the sparrow's silhouette. "Might put a little flap back into your wings, mightn't it? Big chunk of wheaty stuff like this."

Stan looked down at him with an expression of infinite piety. "I may be the last one left, Max, but I'm not ready to go just yet. Not right now, anyway."

"Just a thought," Max shrugged off the damp. "There's been no humans leaving their food about here," he explained.

"Well someone's left a flapping great rat over by the gurgling hole," replied Stan pointing with his beak.

"Don't mess me about," snapped Max.

"I can see the tail from here, mate. Dead as yesterday, it has to be said. And only a little more frozen than what I am."

"You wouldn't joke about a thing like that, would you, Stan?" Max's voice was steely, although the hunger shrieked within him.

"I'm doing you a favour," protested the sparrow.

"Why?"

"Well, I'm taking your mind off me, aren't I?" admitted Stan.

"But it's there alright. Big, dead and nasty. Head down in some brown icy by the gurgling hole."

Max tried to smell for it. But the cold, the ice and the poisoned breath of the coughing boxes had blanked out the smell of any dead flesh. He'd have to go on trust, if he went at all. Round here, going on trust usually proved fatal.

Still, being realistic in the circumstances, who could afford to ignore a frozen rat?

"Alright Stan," he said, "I'll give it a go."

"You're not doing me any favours," chirruped the sparrow, hopping across the rim of the rotting food box to turn his back on Max.

"I'm leaving you alone, Stan," reminded Max as he edged out from beside the soft, stripy thing, "for the time being. But if there's nothing out there, you'll wish the cat had got you too."

Stan hopped back across the box to looked down at him.

"When you can fly, Max, you might be a worry," he called down. "Right now, though, you're just another furry jerk with his belly stuck in the icy, aren't you?"

And he darted off. Leaving Max to the creeping darkness and a lost, dead rat.

Max moved out at once. In this light there was no good time to break cover – the most you could hope for was to take whatever was waiting for you by surprise. He splashed and scrabbled through the slush towards the gurgling hole.

Although the frozen mulch half concealed him, he knew there were any number of ways he could die out here – crushed by a coughing box, crash-dived by an owl or a hawk or simply drowned in some ice filled pit he'd forgotten about.

He moved on steadily, nosing through the ice and the darkness towards where his memory had fixed the gurgling hole, feeling the vitality being frozen out of him with every skidding step he took. His hearing picked up the noise of seeping water first, and then he scrabbled upon it.

The gurgling hole was too clogged by debris and slush to gurgle now. But it did boast a magnificent dead rat. Stan had been true to his word.

Max gave it a good nose. Sodden, frozen and with the guts pressed out of it by a long gone coughing box, this rat was a real meal. He was looking round for a vantage point to tug it to when death landed muscularly in front of him, in the murderous form of Brian and Ray, the crow family firm.

Instantaneously Max backed into the stone kerb above the gurgling hole, placing its shiny, slippery rungs between him and the menacing birds. If they rushed in for the kill now a skid could give him a fraction of a second. A fraction of a chance.

Looming at him across the gurgling hole, Brian planted both feet firmly in the icy. The cold just didn't seem to touch him. The crow looked at Max for some time, sparing only one eye for this, and then spoke with malignant relish, "Max, old son, I'd say you're in the wrong place at the wrong time."

"The wrong time. The wrong place," snapped his brother Ray. He gave the rat corpse a vicious, proprietorial stab with his glinting beak. "And the wrong rat."

"Don't often see you out this late, Brian," said Max, in an effort to slow things down. "Specially in this kind of light."

"Nasty bit of weather," agreed Brian and he eased his wing feathers suddenly. Max knew better than to flinch.

"Nasty," echoed Ray flipping the rat's frozen tail with his beak into a small, sad, sodden wave at Max in what might be his last moments. "Cold and nasty."

"Unlike you, Max," Brian observed, his eye probing deep into Max's.

"He's warm and tasty," Ray's shoulders jerked as he caught his brother's drift. "Warm and tasty, Brian." He gave the matter more thought. "Go down a treat with that rat, wouldn't he?"

"You're getting Ray all excited." Brian stepped back, but Max knew the attack was about to begin. "And everybody knows too much excitement can be very bad for your health."

"You've got a good rat there, Brian," said Max carefully, his eyes flicking from beak to beak, "and right now you can eat it with both eyes open. You come for me and at least one of you will get your head chewed out."

"Well hard," Ray sneered into the mist above him. "Don't know he's already dead, does he, Brian?"

"I've already taken a sparrowhawk. You know that." Max concentrated on Brian, trying to maintain a reasoning conversation.

"Just a baby, I heard."

"Tore his wing out, Brian," Max reminded him. "Now you might take me here, but you'll limp away crippled."

"Warm and tasty!" shrieked Ray.

"I'll ground you, Brian. It may be the last thing that I do, but I'll ground you."

Brian shifted the weight on his feet. Max watched the eyes as the crow reasoned it all out. They had to be ravenous to be out this late in the day. But they could live with a night's hunger. They couldn't live with a shattered wing. Max's life depended on that.

"Ray," Brian began quietly, and his brother scuttled up beside him.

"Wassat, my old china?" said Ray.

Brian looked long and hard at Max. "Take him!" he snarled and the brothers drew up for the attack.

The big blue coughing box slewed into the lay-by throwing out an airborne wave of icy filth. Brian and Ray stretched every desperate sinew to take off before it, leaving the deluge to break over Max.

This, however, was one attack he could withstand, he thought as he fought to retain his balance. No slashing beaks. Just watery cold.

For once a coughing box had done him a favour but he gave it little thought as he splashed and scrambled his way across the lay-by, just outside the treacherous gleam of the pale yellow eyes, to fling himself down again beside the human soft stripy thing.

Peering back at the gurgling hole he could just make out the shapes of Brian and Ray descending, wings beating wildly to tear their anger out on the dead rat.

That rat was definitely a no-go area, but there might be

some fresh leavings in the rotting food box from these new human arrivals.

A big, fat male human stumbled out of the door at the front of the blue coughing box, bringing with him an arid smell of smoke and a burst of complex human noise.

"I'm not driving round all night. I'm bloody dumping it here," he shouted.

A female squawked at him from inside the box.

"It's a lay-by. There's laws."

The big male stormed round to the back of the coughing box and pulled the two doors open. "There's a bin, isn't there? The council'll shift it. If there's a bin. Got to."

"Should've gone to the dump," replied the female, unimpressed.

"Dump's still closed," shouted the male, as he dragged a squat and strangely silver firtree out of the back of the van. "Poxy Christmas. Goes on forever."

He threw the little firtree towards Max by the rotting food box. Max ducked as it bounced off the human soft stripy thing and landed in the gutter. He noted with some pleasure that the impact had distracted Brian and Ray from their rat again, but the human was already hauling two big bags of black shiny out and tossing them after the tree.

They landed with a curious jangling sound between the tree and where Max was huddled.

"I'm sick of it," announced the big male. "Pig sick of it."

"Not as sick as I am!" shouted the female, with sudden venom. "You've done nothing but drink and moan, all the way through. No wonder the kids are all upset."

"You done nothing but stick your head in the box and nag," retorted the big male, closing one of the back doors with a deafening slam. Brian and Ray took off again.

"All that fuss about some little kittens," jeered the female.

The male shouted through the inside of the coughing box and his terrible anger echoed around the mist shrouded night.

"Normal people might get one cat for Christmas. But not you, oh no. Only a loony like you tries to land us with five bloody kittens!"

Bloody kittens, thought Max and a spasm of hunger wracked him.

"You broke their hearts."

"I let them keep one, didn't I? I found bloody homes for the others, didn't I?"

"So you say," spat the female. "I know Pete and Eileen have taken one 'cos I asked them myself. And I got Auntie Peg to pick up one for the play school. But God knows what you've done with the other two."

"They're alright, don't you worry!" shouted the male as he pulled out a smaller bag from the dark cave inside the coughing box. "I'll be bloody glad when I'm back at work," he muttered to himself as he carried this third bag over towards Max's refuge.

Max's heart slammed in panic against his rib cage and the male approached him gingerly holding the bag. He shrank back into the icy slush until just his eyes and nose remained out of the freezing muck.

The big fat male set the bag down gently on the human soft stripy thing.

"Stop pottering about," the female called over to him. "It's freezing in here."

"Keep your hair on," he bawled over his shoulder, and then he turned back to talk softly to something inside the bag as he fiddled in it with his stumpy fingers. "You'll be alright, here. No problem. There's loads of mice about and everything. You'll be great." And then sharper, "There's nothing I can do."

He returned awkwardly to the back of the coughing box and slammed the last door shut. Then he scrabbled in the front. After a beat the box coughed into life and lurched out of the lay-by.

But Max had no interest in the coughing box, now it was leaving. No fear. No apprehension. Because just two feet in front of him on the human soft stripy thing, the black bag began to wriggle about and out of its opening tottered a tiny kitten.

"Mum?" said the kitten tentatively. "You there, Mum?"

"Wait for me, Simon, wait." Another little voice came from inside the bag. "Is Mum there? Mum?"

"It's just more dark, Emily," said Simon, pushing cautiously with his feet against the human soft stripy thing. "And wet, and cold. Mum?"

Emily staggered out of the bag and fell against him. They clouted and pulled at each other as they stumbled to their feet.

"Get off!"

"You get off!"

"You!"

"No you!"

The abruptly they stopped and stared at the world in wonder.

"Mum?"

"Mum? Look at all this stripy, Simon."

"Let's catch it, shall we?"

"And bite it!"

"I'm going first, look."

Max raised his head above the slush in disbelief. No animal believes in miracles. He stole a glance towards the gurgling hole and could just make out the flapping and stamping as Brian and Ray tore apart their frozen rat.

He was definitely ahead of the game here, he thought as he turned back to the midwinter banquet that the human had delivered to him.

Little plump kittens. Things were looking up. Max poised for the spring.

The vixen came on the run from nowhere to take Emily up by the head. She tossed the kitten expertly into the air to break its back, at the same time calling sharply over her shoulder. "Beverly! There's another one here. Go on, girl."

"I don't believe it," Beverly replied delightedly as she stood over Simon. She was almost fully grown herself. Max

sunk back into the slush again. "Mum, I just do not believe it!"

Simon wobbled slightly as the fox cub sniffed at him. "Have you seen all this stripy?" he said brightly. "Fancy a play with it?"

"Come on Bev, we ain't got all barking night." Emily's body muffled the vixen's voice. But her impatience was clear as she trotted away on long journey back to the set.

"Mum?" said Simon, once more for luck. "Mum?"

"Bev!" the vixen barked, unseen and moving further.

"Comin' Mum!" Beverley shouted back, and with an adolescent bad humour she took a savage bite into Simon, and splashed away with him into the filthy evening.

Max steadied his anger. Anger wasn't going to feed him.

He stuck his head under the human soft stripy thing, trying to keep some airspace between it and the damp ground. This was now his only option.

He listened intently for the tell tale scrabbling of frantic mice. Incredibly, somewhere not too far away, someone was talking.

"Breed. We've got to breed," said Uncle George.

Max edged towards the noise.

# Chips Hardy

Chips Hardy is a British Comedy Award winner and has produced and written for television and the theatre. He was born in 1950 in Ealing, London. He went to Cambridge, and threw himself into *The Very Modern Novel*, *Situationism* and other more established university theatricals. In 1972 he flirted with BBC Drama and subsequently veered off, into advertising. He is now international Creative Director for JWT. Hardy's screenplay *Acts of Charity* is in development. A play, *Blue on Blue*, which was showcased at the Latchmere Theatre by Shotgun is soon to go national tour.

# Oscar Grillo

Oscar Grillo is a celebrated animation director, specializing in commercials. He was born in 1943 in Buenos Aires, Argentina, and now resides in London. Since 1960 Grillo has been an influential cartoonist working on illustrations for books such as *Faust*, *The World is Round*, *The Private Diaries of Rembrandt*, *Gulliver Travels* and *I Malavoglia*. In 1980 he won the golden palm at Cannes for his film *Seaside Women* which was also nominated for BAFTA. In 2001 he worked with the art department of Pixar on the visual development for *Monsters, Inc.* After working for more than forty years in animation Oscar has taken a sabbatical from animating and has concentrated mostly on books illustration and painting, having exhibited in England and abroad.

Oscar Grillo is currently working on illustrating *The Tempest* for Can of Worms's *Graphic Shakespeare* series. www.GraphicShakespeare.com.

To view more of Oscar Grillo's work, visit his weblog at www.grillomation.blogspot.com.